I0522865

THE
DARK
LEDGER

OTHER BOOKS IN
THE HAUNTING MYSTERIES OF
MAGGIE STYLES SERIES:

THE GHOST OF BETHEL CHURCH

THE DARK LEDGER

Wil Hodge

This is a work of fiction. Names, characters, businesses, places, and events are either the products of the author's imagination or are used in a fictitious manner. Any resemblance to actual persons, living or dead, or actual events is purely coincidental.

Copyright © 2013, 2023 by Wilton D. Hodge

All rights reserved. No part of this book may be reproduced or transmitted in any form or by any means, electronic or mechanical, including photocopying, recording, or any information storage and retrieval system, without permission in writing from author.

ISBN: 978-0-9894848-0-0 - Paperback
eISBN: 978-0-9894848-1-7 - ePub
eISBN: 978-0-9894848-2-4 - mobi

These ISBNs are the property of BookLogix for the express purpose of sales and distribution of this title. BookLogix is not responsible for the writing or editing of this book. The content of this book is the property of the copyright holder only. BookLogix does not hold any ownership of the content of this book and is not liable in any way for the materials contained within. The views and opinions expressed in this book are the property of the Author/Copyright holder, and do not necessarily reflect those of BookLogix.

Printed in the United States of America

♾This paper meets the requirements of ANSI/NISO Z39.48-1992 (Permanence of Paper)

Cover photography: Amelia Hodge
Cover model (front and back): Kourtney Shales
Cover layout: Ryan Almario

www.wilhodge.com

021523

This book is dedicated to my daughter,
AMELIA HODGE

*"You only go through this life once.
Be yourself. You are the only one who can be."*

I'd like to thank everyone who helped me
keep the fire burning while writing this book.

AMELIA HODGE, KARLA HODGE,
RYAN ALMARIO, YVONNE SHALES,
KOURTNEY SHALES and DONNA DEEB.

Chapter 1

FLAT AND TIRED

The Colorado Mountains spoke to Jack in words meant for him alone. The majestic whispers came to him subliminally as the miles passed beneath him and his catalog laden SUV. It would be only a short while now until the night lights from downtown Denver would beckon him to stop for the night. As a small bear appeared in his headlights, he slowed to watch it waddle to the woods along the side of the road. It was a welcome sight. Life. He'd taken it for granted for the last eight hours.

Jack Reynolds came from a long line of salesmen. His grandfather sold carpet, his father sold carpet and Jack, being the rebel, sold prefabricated log cabins. These were real log homes that were built in a factory in Ellijay, Georgia and trucked all over the country. They could be re-constructed in a day or two, depending on the size, then ready for utilities to be hooked up shortly after. He was on a roll as he'd sold two in six weeks. Not a very good roll, but still he remained confident that Colorado would be a gold mine for the cabins. Fishermen, miners, campsites and resorts all needed cheap living space. Yep, Jack had a car packed with optimism, and then, his left rear tire blew.

"Shit!" Jacked barked as he looked in his side mirror at his obviously flat tire flopping under the weight of his car. It's funny how even in the dark a flat tire always looks like it makes you feel; flat and tired.

Jack pulled off the road and got out to inspect the

damage. His digital dash clock read 2:08 in the morning and he was still quite a way from Denver with his car packed with catalogs and wood samples for the cabins. To get to his spare tire he'd have to unpack his car there in the dark, get the spare and jack out, then change the now pitiful looking scrap of rubber that lay wrapped around his tire rim. He just didn't have the initiative.

Sleeping in his car on the side of the road was not something Jack had counted on. He had meetings set up for the next day that he didn't want to miss and to show up looking like he'd slept in his car all night might be worse than not showing up at all. At the moment he didn't care, he was exhausted. He was about to crawl into the front seat and put the seat back when a pair of headlights could be seen coming up the road behind him. He strained to see through the brightness when the car began to slow. The lights blinded him as he held his hand up in front of his eyes. Then, like a carnival ride at the circus, blue lights began to swirl. "I don't believe it. A cop when you need one."

Jack could now make out the word "Sheriff" written on the door as it opened. A tall deputy got out with, "Evenin'. Having some trouble?"

Jack let out a sigh of relief as he said, "Man, you got that right. I got a load of catalogs back there and my spare is underneath it all."

The deputy shined his flashlight down on the shredded tire and said, "Looks like your rim's gone too. Sorry buddy, but you gotta mess back here."

Jack agreed and after they both concluded that changing a tire on a mountain road at what was now 2:12 in the morning wasn't the best way to go, he found himself sitting in the front seat of the Sheriff's car as they drove along the mountain road.

"You a salesman?"

"Yeah," Jack lazily replied, like it was an answer he'd rather not admit.

"What do you sell?"

"Cabins. Prefabricated cabins from Georgia. Good ones too. Made from sturdy Georgia pine with a mother's love."

The deputy smiled at Jack's candor. "Sell any lately?"

"Yeah man, I'm on a roll. I sold two in six weeks."

"Well hotdamn!" The deputy exclaimed. Then the two men burst out laughing. Jack laughed from frustration, the deputy laughed from sympathy, but it was a well-timed moment in a night that cabin salesman Jack Reynolds would love to forget.

The deputy held out his hand and said, "Name's Sam Hecker."

Shaking the sheriff's offered hand, "Jack Reynolds. Pleasure. You sure came along at the right time, I tell you."

"Do cabin salesmen drink beer?" The deputy said with a slight tilt of his head.

"Right now, they do," Jack responded.

With that Jack could see lights coming from the side of the road up ahead. As they got closer a sign read "The Grizzly Beer Trap." The deputy pulled in the small gravel parking lot and the patrol car came to a rest next to a wrecker.

"Your lucky night," the sheriff began. "Pete's here. He can go get your car and take it down the mountain for you."

"Did you know he'd be here?" Jack asked, still looking at the made to order wrecker.

"I had a feeling. We both get off at 2:00. We've been getting a beer after work here for thirteen years now. Pete's my brother."

As Jack got out of the patrol car he could see "Hecker's Wrecker" written on the side of the wrecker door. "Nice to have a brother with a wrecker." Jack then noticed the place across the street. It looked like an old barn with all sorts of "Antiques" signs in the front.

"What's that over there? Looks like a barn sale."

"That's Maggie Styles' Antique Barn. She gets shit from all over the country. Sells most of it on the Internet. Antiques, old crap that barely works. Beats me why folks buy that stuff."

As they walked in the bar Jack asked the deputy, "She got any old tools?"

"Tools? What kind of tools? There's a hardware store just down the mountain that opens in the morning. What do you want tools for?"

"It's not for me. It's for my boss. His birthday's coming up and he collects old tools. I bet he's got over a hundred old saws, levels, and sanders. The man's got at least twenty-five hammers from the 1800's. No lie."

"Oh, looking to do a little brown nosing, huh?" The sheriff laughed. "I get it. Maggie opens up around ten. You can go there after breakfast. You're not going anywhere else with that tire."

"I don't understand," Jack replied. "After breakfast? You mean we're staying here all night?"

"Not me, you are. That is unless you want to sleep out here in the parking lot. Pete's got a spare room he lets folks that can't drive home stay in. It's real clean and all. His wife sees it's suitable for guests, if you can call them that."

"Pete's wife? She ride with him in the wrecker?"

"She does sometimes. She also happens to own this bar."

Jack looked into the bar and back at the wrecker. Both of them said at the same time once more, "Well hotdamn!"

Chapter 2

WALL OF SHAME

Jack woke up the next morning in a little room that was nothing more than a glorified closet. It was so dark he couldn't see more than a few inches in front of him. He reached in his pocket for his cell phone to check in on reality and illuminate the room, but it wasn't there. He checked the other pocket, and then realized his phone was in his car on the side of the road. Jack jumped up from the bed and hit his head on the low angled ceiling, then fell back in agony. Somewhere in the distance he heard the faint sound of an old Waylon Jennings song he'd forgotten.

He slowly picked himself up and reached for the low doorknob. As the door opened, a flood of sunlight met him as he grabbed his eyes with his hands. Walking into the bar, he looked around and noticed about fifteen people casually drinking and eating breakfast, acting like he wasn't even there.

"Morning!" came a familiar voice. Jack looked up to see Pete's wife, Grace, standing behind the counter holding a pot of coffee. "You want a cup?" she asked.

"Or ten," Jack whispered as he slid onto a barstool. "What time is it?"

As Grace poured the coffee into a cup, Jack looked up to see her pointing at a bucking bronco hanging on the wall. "What the hell is that?" Jack said squinting to see what it was she was pointing at.

"It's a clock," Grace answered as the coffee poured.

Jack couldn't focus yet. "What's it say?"

"Ten forty," Grace chuckled as she stood back from the bar.

Jack got his bearings straight and then asked, "What day is it?"

Grace started to smile and whispered, "Thursday."

If Jack was drunk when he went to bed, he was suddenly sober now. "Ten forty! I'm a dead man. I had a meeting at nine this morning. Do you have a phone?"

The next fifteen minutes found Jack trying to see well enough to read a phone book as he looked for a number of a place he'd forgotten the name. "All my numbers are in my phone in my car. By the way, where is Pete? He's gotta go get my car."

Grace just shook her head. "Pete went after your car this morning and already has it at the shop down the road. They'll have you going by noon. Pete called an hour ago to tell me to tell you that when you woke up. You want some food for that head?"

Jack surrendered to the situation. He was screwed. He'd missed his meeting, had no cell phone, and was at the mercy of a woman in an apron with bad coffee and a husband who drove a wrecker. "This sucks!"

"Go get a shower out back. It'll make you feel better," Grace said pointing to the back door.

"Where out back?" Jack said looking confused.

With that, Grace led Jack to the makeshift outdoor shower stall behind the bar. There were marks on the side of the stall that seemed to be keeping a count of something.

"What are those for?" Jack asked.

"Nothing. Just helps us keep track of how many people we've saved up here. You're not the first, you know." She walked over to the stall and took a crayon down off the window ledge then put another mark on the side.

"See you later," she smirked as she turned to walk back into the bar.

"This is crazy," Jack admitted as he stepped into the stall and began to disrobe. He was relieved that only his head, shoulders and feet could be seen from the outside.

As the cold mountain water hit his face, Jack recoiled. Letting the water run over him, he felt the life coming back into his body. He turned his back to the water, opened his eyes and FLASH! He looked up through a big dot in front of him to see Grace standing there with a camera and laughing.

"It's for the wall," she said, as she went back into the bar.

"Wall? What wall?" Jack asked, as his focus returned.

When Jack came back into the bar, Grace led him to a back room to see a wall with a bulletin board full of pictures of men and women standing in that little shower looking like hell. "You're famous now, Jack." she said proudly. "There you are on the Grizzly Beers' Wall of Shame. Ha!"

All Jack could do was hang his head and slowly start to laugh. "Wall of Shame, huh?"

Grace pointed to the window and said, "So is she!"

Jack looked out the window and saw an attractive woman in the parking lot across the street.

"That's Maggie. Sells old shit. She says one day she's even going to try to sell me."

Jack was mesmerized. The woman had a simple elegance that seemed out of place in the mountains.

"She's a looker isn't she?" Grace admitted, walking back behind the bar.

"Yeah, she's that alright," Jack had to admit. "She got any old tools over there?"

"If it's old, she's probably got it. She's been collecting that stuff for years. She bought the place from her whacko dad. Go see what she's got." Grace smirked as she turned away.

Jack glanced back with a slight smile. "I'll do that."

Chapter 3

I'M JACK REYNOLDS

Jack got himself in the best shape possible and walked across the gravel parking lot to Maggie Styles' Antique Barn. As he walked up to the old building, he could almost feel its contents of mostly aged and forgotten furniture, pictures in old frames and dusty relics of a time long gone.

The big barn doors were opened wide. Jack felt like he was going into a sideshow at the county fair as there were indefinable objects everywhere. He had no idea what half of it was. This was a funhouse for the senses all right. Then, in the middle of all that rust, dust and curiosity came a voice, "Well, hello there. Can I help you find something?"

Startled at the unexpected greeting, Jack shuddered a little and turned to see the owner standing next to him. "Hi, I'm Maggie Styles." As he looked into the face of the woman, he realized he had forgotten to breathe.

Jack had spent a lot of time studying greetings. It's a salesman's first impression. Too much enthusiasm would kill a sale before it got off the ground. Too little would make the potential client think the salesman wasn't worthy of their time and cut the meeting short. Just the right "hello" was what was needed here. With that, Jack took a breath, turned, and as he reached out his hand to Maggie's, his shirtsleeve caught the edge of a lamp sitting on a table next to him and sent the lamp crashing to the wooden floor.

Maggie had obviously been in that same situation before. She stepped back, looked at the destroyed lamp on the ground and shrugged. "Actually, I never liked that lamp anyway. It's been here five years. I'm glad it's gone."

"I'll pay for it!" Jack clumsily offered, trying to get his salesmanship back to form.

"Forget it. Like I said, it was a piece of junk anyway. Don't worry about it. Is there anything else in here that you'd like to break?"

All Jack could do was sigh. "At least let me clean it up for you."

There was something about Jack that Maggie liked. He had tried to make a good first impression but an untimely event had shown her a side of him that sometimes takes a while to reveal in a relationship. Here she had just met the man, and already she was further down the road with him than she had been in a long time with anyone.

"The broom and shovel are over there. As you can see, I keep them handy." She watched Jack walk over and pick up the broom. He did some really bad swordplay with it as he came back to do battle with the broken lamp. "On guard!" Jack said laughingly as he began to sweep the shards of broken glass into a pile on the floor.

"I'm Jack Reynolds, by the way." Then he went into a radio announcer voice that sounded somewhere between Gable and Bogart. "Other than being a master lamp smasher, I'm actually a salesman of fine prefabricated cabins. You can be impressed at any time."

"Oh, I see. A traveling salesman looking for a punch line," Maggie coyly replied.

"Ouch! Man, you are cruel." It was clear Jack had his work cut out for him. It was funny, he wasn't trying to sell her anything, he wasn't looking for a romantic mountain liaison, he simply, unexplainably, wanted her to like him. This out of place woman here on Mount Random in somewhere Colorado had his full attention, and he really wondered why. He decided right there to name it, "Maggie Mountain."

"So, what brought you to my door, Jack Reynolds? You just happened to drive by and took a chance I'd have what you were looking for?"

"Actually, I was driving up the mountain last night and my car…."

Maggie stopped him with, "Don't tell me. Your car broke down and you needed a place to spend the night, so, here you are on my doorstep. You are truly a walking traveling salesman joke."

"That's not altogether true," Jack said, looking over at The Grizzly Beer. "My car did break down. A deputy came along and took me to the bar over there in the middle of the night. He said his sister-in-law owned the place and…" Maggie stopped him again.

"So, how'd it look?"

Jack stepped back and said, "How'd what look?"

"How'd your picture look?" Maggie said with a 'gotcha' tone in her voice.

Jack was now rattled. He realized she must have seen more guys than he could count come over from the bar looking for whatever. Probably her. This was all part of a scenario that had played out many times.

"You're on the Wall of Shame, aren't you?" Maggie smirked.

"Yeah. Busted. Guilty as charged. How'd you know that?"

"Grace has had her fun with that camera. My picture is on the bottom row. I gave up trying to take it down. I got hammered in there on my birthday a few years ago. Live and learn. She got me big time in that shower."

Jack felt like he was at last out of the frying pan with the conversation. "Well, I gotta say I feel better now knowing I wasn't as stupid as I thought. So, tell me, which notch are you?"

Maggie laughed and looked down then up at Jack. "One of the first. You going to go back and stare at my notch?"

Jack stopped and studied the line she'd just given him, and then all he could come up with was, "Probably."

"Let's get to it Mr. Jack Reynolds. What's got you in my barn?"

"I'm looking for…"

"Yes….." Maggie said mockingly, like she was hanging on his every word.

"Old tools. Preferably from the early 1800's or before."

"Anything in particular?" Maggie started. "A hammer? A screw….driver maybe?"

Jack could see the comedy in her eyes and loved her sexy banter. Thinking he too could play the game, he looked at her and finished sweeping the glass. Then he said in a slow and sultry voice, "Where do you want it?"

Maggie recoiled and stepped back. "Excuse me?"

"Where do you want…the glass?" Jack asked, while holding the old shovel full of the broken lamp.

Maggie had to top his innuendo. She smiled and said, "Put it in my can."

Jack looked up surprised as she said, "It's over there."

Jack walked, grinning, to the overflowing trashcan. Maggie asked, "So, did you really come in to look for tools or did you simply have an uncontrollable urge to break a lamp?"

"No, really, I am looking for old tools. You see, my boss, (back into his radio voice) Seth Holiday, owner of Holiday Cabins in Ellijay, Georgia, is a collector of old tools."

Maggie laughed. "You should be a disc jockey with that voice."

"Well, I have been told I have a face for radio." Jack said with a big smile.

"A face for radio? I think you may be a little modest, Jack Reynolds. You really came in here looking for old tools?"

"No kidding," Jack began. "My boss has a garage full of them. Some are really rare. They just look like old tools to me. Anyway, his birthday is coming up. I thought if I could find him something it would be nice to give it to him then."

"Oh, doing a little brown nosin'. I get it," Maggie said in another 'gotcha!' tone.

"That's what the deputy said. That's not it. Seth's actually a great guy. We're all like family back home. There are nine of us and we've been together four years now. Sold fifty-six cabins and counting."

"Fifty-six, huh? You sell all those?" Maggie asked.

"No. Not all of them, just three," Jack said hanging his head looking for girl sympathy.

"Three? Out of fifty-six?"

Jack looked around the room and said, "Tools? Old tools?"

As Jack and Maggie walked around the barn, he was amazed at all the antiquities. "How long did it take you find all this?"

"I didn't find it all. I bought the business years ago from my dad who was looking to retire to Florida. Said he was tired of the snow season up here. He lives down around Jacksonville now with his girlfriend. Happy as a clam."

"He has a girlfriend? That's great! How old is your dad?"

"Dad's fifty-eight now. He's kind of a hippie. He never grew up, really. He's one of a kind, and his girlfriend is just like him. It's a circus because she's as odd as he his. It was love at first sight, according to Dad at least."

"The lady across the street said he was a whack job. Sounds like they had some time together," Jack concluded as he motioned to the bar across the road.

Maggie had to laugh. "Dad and Grace have been going at it for years. They are the kind of people that constantly complain about each other being weird or crazy, but they are the ones that come running to the other's side at the first sign of something wrong. They love each other in their own way; it's just between them. They've been name calling each other for years."

"Sounds like a marriage. Were they ever a couple, or something like that?" Jack asked.

"Lord, no!" Maggie scoffed. "Not that either will admit anyway."

"Where'd he get all this?" Jack asked not knowing where to look next.

"From everywhere. Auctions, yard sales. Took him thirty years to find it all. I saw a gold mine in it. He never took any of this online because he's not into computers at all and doesn't even have e-mail. He says the government is watching everything online, which they probably are. I have sold more through the net than I ever do here. UPS comes twice a week. It's lucrative if you know where to advertise. And I do."

"You just quit your life and moved up here to sell antiques? What did you do before you were an antique dealer?" Jack had to know.

Maggie leaned back on an old chest of drawers and dared a, "Guess."

Jack was once more in the hot seat. A wrong answer could insult her. An over qualified answer might make her feel inferior. Now, his salesman training was on the line here. He really liked her, so he took a deep breath and answered, "Computers. You did something in software."

"Why would you say that? Do I look like a nerd?"

"Nope, not at all. You just seem to have an air of brilliance about you and you know the net. It's rare I meet someone I can't put my finger on. Am I close?" Jack asked, as he braced for the result of his questioning.

"History professor," Maggie confirmed, as a matter of fact.

"No! You were a teacher?" Then he stopped, took a step back and gave her a boyish grin and said, "I'll bet you were great. Where'd you teach?"

Maggie answered in a southern belle's accent, "I have a master's degree in American History from the University of Tennessee." Then she laughed. "After I graduated one of my professors retired and a job came open. They offered it to me, and I jumped on it. I was there a few years, and decided to try something else. Dad wanted to get out of here, so I bought the place from him and have been here ever since."

Jack was fascinated. "I'd have never figured it. You, a professor."

"I'd have never pegged you for a salesman. People are funny creatures, aren't they? Now let's look for your tool. Shouldn't be hard to find." Maggie smiled and began to motion for Jack to follow her.

She was running on a cruise control she wasn't used to. Maggie had just let him in, and that hadn't happened in a long time. Here she had just met this guy and was already telling him privileged information. Yet, there she had been, babbling on like an old maid at a revival.

After a stroll around the path that led through the aisles of tables, chairs, mirrors and such, Jack and Maggie came full circle to where they started.

"Looks like I'm outta luck. No tools." Jack said with a sigh.

Maggie didn't want Jack to leave yet. He seemed smart, funny and had a great laugh. He reminded her of her first real boyfriend, someone she sometimes looked for when she went back to her home in Tennessee but had never seen. There weren't any men on the mountain she was interested in, but here was someone that moved her a little. She didn't know why just yet, but she wanted to know more about him. Then she said it. Totally out of character for her, but she had to know. "You married?"

Jack stepped back and looked at Maggie with a "hello!" grin and said "Nope. You?" Maggie smiled and said, "Nope. Not even close. If you want to see more stuff, there's some in the building behind here. It's really dirty out there and I haven't been through any of that stuff since I bought the place. I don't know what's there. To be honest, it's spooky. I don't much care for spiders, dark places, you know, things that scare little girls."

The sunlight hit Jack and Maggie as they walked out the back door. Both commented on the day. It was hard not to. Even for Maggie, the Colorado sky was awe-inspiring.

"I never get used to this," she said. "I see it every day and it still wows me."

"I gotta agree. I rolled in last night and it's a new ballgame in the daylight. I could get used to this. I'm more a mountain person than a beach guy," Jack said while breathing the fresh air.

"Me too," Maggie confessed. "I feel out of place at the beach. It's hot. Though it's great to go every few years, I'd rather be here. Can't explain it. Ahh, here we go. Out building number one. I haven't been in here in two years. God knows what we'll find. Maybe your tool!"

Jack looked at Maggie with both an admiration and a sense of delight. Something was familiar about her. It was like he wasn't having to get to know her, but only remember her.... from somewhere.

Maggie opened the creaky door to a small building stacked halfway to the ceiling with what looked like the remains of a neighborhood yard sale. Boxes were scattered everywhere as dust fell like fine snow. "Jesus. Where do you start?" Jack said, while looking at all the boxes.

"You start where you start," Maggie said, walking up to the first box and opening it. "Here you go. Box number one. Not many tools here. Only about a hundred more to go. Watch for spiders. I hate spiders."

As Maggie turned to walk away Jack said, "Hey, you leaving me out here?"

"Hell yeah. I got a UPS truck coming in an hour and need to get an order ready. Just go through the stuff and see what you find. Let me know if you find anything interesting. Hope you find your tool."

Jack watched Maggie walk away toward the barn with admiration as he sighed and said under his breath, "Good job, God." Maggie was indeed a pretty lady.

The boxes held mostly stuff that could be found in a garbage pile by the side of the road had it not ended up here. It was a graveyard for the obscure household item such as toasters, the burner from a stove that had long ago seen its last pan of biscuits, a light switch from an old house somewhere; you name it. Relics that pre-dated any indication there would ever be a Home Depot were about all there were.

Then, from under a box in the back, he saw a handle. "Yes!" Jack began to move the boxes out of the way to get to it as dust flew up with every motion he made. At last, he came to an old trunk sitting on top of a double-handled saw. These saws were popular with lumber mills back before there were chain saws. The trunk sitting on it was heavy. He tried to move it, but it seemed like it was going nowhere.

Just when he was about to give up, he heard, "Hey! You in here?"

"Yeah!" Jack yelled from the back.

"Your car's ready!" It was Pete Hecker.

Jack looked up to see Pete walking back to him.

"Bunch of shit. You know what you're looking for out here? Maggie said tools?" Jack stepped back from the trunk. "Yeah. I found an old saw here but this trunk is on top of it. Can you give me a hand and help me get it off?"

Jack and Pete slowly moved the trunk off the old saw. It was a long lumberjack saw all right. It was a little rusty, but still in decent shape.

"Man, this is cool! I need this for my boss." Jack held up the long saw and it flexed and bowed in the middle.

"How you going to get it home?" Pete wondered. "It looks longer than your car can take. There's no room for it."

Jack had to say that Pete was right. Then they heard, "I can ship it." They turned to see Maggie walking up. "UPS will ship darn near anything. Nice saw. That what you want?"

"Yeah, I guess. I was hoping for something smaller, like a plane or an old drill."

Pete stepped back and said, "I'll leave you to it. Your car is at the bottom of the mountain at Tony's garage. Can't miss it. I'll give you a ride, but we've got to go now. I have a car to tow off the side of the road ten miles out."

Jack looked at his saw and then looked at Maggie. It was the end of his time with her and he really liked her. She was smart, funny and had something he hadn't seen in a woman. He didn't want to leave yet. Their eyes met and he felt like she had the same sense of wanting to know him. There was something there and they both felt it. He knew it, so he threw her a look. An "I don't want to leave yet" look. Then Maggie said, "I'll give him a ride." Jack felt a wave of relief come over him.

Pete turned to leave. "Your call Miss Maggie. I'm outta here. Jack, you can pay Tony down the mountain. My fees are in there with the bill. Good luck, partner."

Pete turned to walk away and then stopped. "Oh yea, nice picture." Pete glanced at Maggie and they both smiled. Pete walked away leaving Jack and Maggie in the wake of what had just been acknowledged between them. They were suddenly together. Just like that. He knew it. She knew it. Here in the outbuilding, two people that had known each other for a little more than an hour took a leap. Where it would take them neither one could imagine.

Maggie looked at the saw. "So, this your tool? It's a big one! I'm impressed. Your boss will be a happy man."

Jack smiled and looked down at the very old trunk that stood about three feet high and as wide. It resembled an old pirate chest found at the end of a treasure map where 'X' marked the spot. Jack saw both curiosity and a reason to stay with Maggie longer as he looked at that trunk.

"What's in there? Anvils? It's heavy as hell," Jack asked, pointing to the trunk.

"It's locked. I know that much. I tried to open it a long time ago but got distracted, I guess. You know anything about locks?" Maggie asked, studying the keyhole.

"I've picked a lock or two in my day. When I'm not selling cabins, I'm actually a British spy. I call in twice a day." Jack went into a display of the aristocracy associated with British Lords. "Reynolds. Jack Reynolds," he said in a mocking James Bond tone.

Maggie was being drawn into Jack's charm and wit with every minute she spent with him. He was handsome, funny and had her in the palm of his hand, a place where she wasn't used to being with any man. But here, in this dusty, shadowy room, she liked it. It was nice to let her guard down and someone else drive for a change.

"Okay, Mister Bond, let's not disappoint the Queen. What'll it take to open this thing?"

"We need a master key. I've opened many a lock with one. It's called a crowbar in layman's terms. Do you think you might have one?" Jack asked.

Maggie smirked at the thought of damaging the possibly valuable trunk, but she was curious about its contents and it was definitely keeping Jack in play for whatever the game turned out to be. "I have one somewhere."

Maggie left for the crowbar and Jack again watched her walk away. When she vanished out of the door, he felt an immediate longing for her and didn't want her out of his sight. "What is it about that woman?" he thought.

Jack then turned his attention to the trunk itself. It was old. There was a personality to it. The strap came across the top in precision and met with the lock in the middle. There were no ornamental carvings on it, just basic wood with brass hardware. It was obviously hand built by someone long ago.

"Here you are, Mister Bond. One master key." Maggie handed Jack the crowbar and he wedged it between the beautifully aged strap that banded the trunk. With one push, it sprang open. "Ho! We're in!" Jack heralded. "Score one for the British Secret Service."

As Jack opened the trunk, they both said at the same time, "Books. Shit!" They laughed at each other's reaction as Jack reached in and pulled out the first book; a very old pamphlet with the pages partially stuck together. Jack picked it up and read: "A View of the Conduct of the Executive in the Foreign Affairs of the United States."

Maggie gasped and stood up. "Oh my God! Let me see that!" Maggie took the pamphlet and studied it. "Jack, this is incredibly rare." She opened the pamphlet carefully as the pages felt the fresh Colorado air. Maggie looked like she had found gold. "I read about this in college. James Monroe wrote it in 1797 and got into some hot water for it politically. There were less than a thousand ever printed. Do you know how valuable this is? It could be worth a fortune. It needs to be in a museum. It's that valuable."

"Yeah, but would anyone pay for it? Who is James Monroe?" Jack said while soaking up her excitement. "Jack, he was the fifth President of The United States, for God's sake. You don't understand. This is the kind of book that goes to auction houses like Sotheby's or Christie's in New York. This could be worth five figures or more." As Maggie looked down at the old books in the trunk her eyes widened. "What else is in there?"

Jack reached in and pulled out other large books that were of some value, but nothing like the prize Maggie was holding as tight as anything she'd ever had. At the bottom of the trunk was a book that seemed older than any he'd seen. It was large. At least a twenty-inch square with a clasp that kept it shut.

Jack pushed on the latch that wouldn't open. He closed the now empty trunk, put the book on top and kept trying. Maggie reached over and said, "It's tricky. I've seen this before. You hold this down and then move this to the side." Jack followed her instructions and the latch popped open.

"Score!" Jack said in triumph.

As he opened the book, they watched as drawings of mechanical schematics saw the light of day. There were pages of sketches done in charcoal and old ink. "What on earth?" Maggie said as she watched the pages slowly go by.

"It looks like drawings of old tools. Look at all these! Somebody must have been an inventor. I've never seen anything like this," Jack said mesmerized.

As Jack went through the drawings, he came to the last pages of the book that were only handwriting. It appeared to be a diary of the inventor's ideas and how the tools would work.

"I think this guy was trying to write out his ideas for some patents, it looks like anyway. This looks like an old ledger for some kind of bookkeeping. I guess this is all he had to draw in. Did they have patents back in…. what? How old is this thing?"

Jack turned the book over and opened it to the back page. Inside the back cover was written, *"This here work is the propty of Daniel T. Blanch, Fredericksburg, Virgina in the year of our Lord 1802."*

"1802!" Jack and Maggie said at the same time. "This is over two hundred years old! And it's about a man and his tools. Maggie, I have to have this."

"What do want with an old man's drawings? Oh, I see. Tools. You want it for your boss, right?" Maggie asked.

"He'd absolutely go crazy for this. It's so him. It's old, dusty and smells bad. Just like him! Sell me this. I'll buy it from you. What's it cost?"

It suddenly dawned on Maggie that she had something that could keep them in touch for a while. It was just an old book, yes, but still it was a timely answer to the question of how she could stay in Jack's life. She looked down at the book clutched in her arms and knew she needed to show both books to her father to find out where the trunk came from. Jack was from Georgia, so she saw a road trip with Jack a possibility. She caught herself thinking total craziness. Here she'd just met this man, and already she felt as both she wanted to run away with him and in the same thought, that she already had. Something was going on here. What ever it was, she knew she was in it for the long haul.

"When do you go back to Georgia?" Maggie asked. "We need to go today."

Jack looked up into the eyes of the woman he knew he had feelings for and never felt such a sense of urgency. Now she was asking him to take her back to Georgia with him.

"Are you out of your mind? I can't go back today. I have a job. I have meetings set up, one of which I've already missed, and the other's in..." It's then Jack jumped back to reality and remembered where he was and why.

"What time is it?" I have a three o'clock meeting! I gotta get my car! My phone is in it and if I lose both my meetings, I'm a dead man. Can you take me to get my car now? I've gotta go!"

Maggie stood there with her arms crossed around the book that she was certain would be worth a small fortune. "Where is your meeting? What town?"

"Vail." Jack sad. "I gotta be in Vail by three or I'm totally screwed."

"Vail!" Maggie screeched. "You've got to be in Vail by three o'clock? Good luck! You'll be lucky to get to Vail in five hours. I'm afraid you really are screwed. No use in trying, you missed it. I'll take you to your car, but you may as well head back. If we leave now, we can get to your car and start back to Florida. It'll take two days, but we've got to go because I have to talk to my father about these books. I have to know where he got them."

"Florida? Who said anything about Florida? I'm from Georgia. North Georgia. Ellijay, Georgia, home of Holiday Cabins where my ass is suddenly on the line. I'm not going to Florida. I'm a salesman, remember? They don't buy many cabins in Florida."

Maggie was looking for a way to make Jack change his mind. She knew he was right and admired his work ethic. He had a responsibility to his company and to himself. After all, how would it look back in Georgia if he happened to call in from Florida when he was supposed to be in Vail, Colorado? She saw his dilemma. Then she made a decision.

"Ok, you have a meeting in Vail at three?"

"That's right." Jack answered. "I had one on the way there at nine this morning and I've missed that one already. I bet my people have left me fifty messages wanting to know where the hell I am."

"Out of those two meetings, how sure were you you'd sell anything? Be honest. Pre-made cabins from Georgia, here in Colorado? I hate to tell you this, but they make cabins in Colorado. Chances are, anyone who wants one has already got one from somebody here. Didn't you know that?"

Jack was becoming frustrated and defensive.

"Where are you going with this? I know my stuff. I researched it. I called ahead and they said they'd see me."

Maggie sighed, "You wouldn't have sold any, Jack. You know it, I know it. Cut the crap. It's a long shot at best."

"What do you know about it? You sell stuff on the net without having to see people or talk…" Maggie cut Jack off mid-sentence. "I'll buy one. You heard me. I'll buy one. You take me to Florida today and you can put me down for one cabin. Raise your total sales to four. Hot damn! What do you say? It'll get you out of the hot seat with your boss, you can write off the trip, you made a sale, and life is good! What do you say?"

Jack was dumbfounded. "Are you serious? You haven't even seen one. You know nothing about it. How can you say you'll buy one?"

"You let me worry about it. You take me to Florida today and I'll buy a cabin. I'll put it near here. I have more land up here than just this place." Maggie stood there in the dusty shed holding what she had concluded would be a major part of her retirement, looking at the man she had decided, right then, would be a part of it, waiting for an answer that would change her life in ways she couldn't calculate. It was a long pause.

Jack knew she was probably right. If she were to agree to buy a cabin, then it would smooth things over back at the factory. She was now in his life. He couldn't explain why, but there she was; his dream girl. Smart, pretty, confident with a walk that he'd never tire of. It all seemed too easy, too tailor-made.

"Why do you need me to take you to Florida? Why can't you just fly down or drive yourself? Or better yet, just call the man."

"Dad doesn't use phones. He thinks the government is listening to everything we say on the telephone. I told you, he still lives in the sixties."

Jack recoiled in disbelief. "What? Are you kiddin' me? He doesn't use a phone or email? How does he communicate with anyone?"

"Pigeons," Maggie said frankly.

Jack looked at her in disbelief. "Pigeons? Oh, come on. This is bullshit!"

"Nope. Dad has been training carrier pigeons for years. That's one of the things he and Grace argued about. Some of his pigeons would sit on the Grizzly Beer sign and bomb her truck. A few still hang around here. They just wait on someone to need something carried, I guess." Maggie looked at Jack's face, which was wide open in disbelief and said, "I'm not making this up, Jack. I told you, Dad's a little odd, but he knows every piece of crap in this place and where he got it. We gotta talk to him and the only way is to go there."

Maggie shrugged in frustration then bent down to pick up another one of the smaller books and her shirt fell loose at the top, giving him a view of her cleavage that was indeed substantial. She rose back up and smiled.

"Let's go to Florida," fell out of his mouth.

Maggie held up her fist in triumph with, "Yes!! I have to stop at the bank before we go. I want to put this pamphlet in a safe deposit box. I don't want anything to happen to it. This is major!"

"I thought you wanted your dad to see it?" Jack said, pondering Maggie's decision.

"He'll know where the trunk came from. Chances are he's never seen this pamphlet anyway, so I don't want to risk it getting lost or damaged. Let's take the ledger. That'll give us something to show him."

Jack agreed. "It's your call and I don't blame you. If that James Monroe thing is indeed what you say it is, it could be worth a haul."

Chapter 4

FIRST CALL TO PARIS

Maggie and Jack arrived at Tony's Auto Shop and saw Jack's repaired car sitting beside the garage. "Thank you, Pete!" Jack was thrilled. After settling with Tony, he got his cell phone from the console showing twenty-two missed calls.

"Somebody out looking for a cabin salesman?" Maggie laughed.

"You have no idea." Jack took a minute to listen to his messages and told Maggie he needed to take a minute for damage control. "I have to make a few calls. Gimme a minute."

"Sure." Maggie sat back in her Jeep.

Jack walked over to the side of the building and looked back at her sitting there like a picture from a men's magazine with "Fantasy" written under it. "What am I doing?"

Jack called his office and heard, "Holiday Cabins, may I help you?"

"Paris?" Jack said.

"Jack! Where have you been? Holiday is about to have the Army out looking for you."

"It's a long story, darlin'. My car broke down on a mountain road; a cop picked me up; and you wouldn't believe it. Better let me talk to him."

"He's pissed, Jack. You missed a meeting this morning and the guy called here upset about it. You need to walk softly here, man."

"I get it. Put me through."

Jack took his phone and held it away from his head and squinted his eyes in preparation for "Jack! Where have you been?" Seth Holiday was, on one hand, Jack's best friend. On the other hand, when business was involved, he was Darth Vader in a suit. Jack could feel Seth's hand on his throat.

"I had a blowout, Seth. Sorry man. No shit. Last night at two o'clock in the morning I had a tire go ballistic on a mountain road in the middle of nowhere. A cop picked me up and took me to some dive bar where I spent the night in a closet with a mattress in it. When I got up, my car had been towed to this auto shop where I am now. My phone was in the console of the car with all my numbers in it. I'm not kiddin' you, it's the God's truth! But you won't believe what happened, I made a sale this morning."

Seth suddenly heard something worth hearing. "You what? You made a sale? To whom?"

"A lady I met. She wants a cabin for some land she has. I'm sorry I missed the pitch in Denver. But hey, I sold something here at least, so the trip wasn't a lost cause." Jack said with a hap-hazard confidence.

"She good for it?" Seth asked now a little more tolerant of Jack's situation.

"Yeah, she's solid." Then Jack glanced back over at Maggie still sitting in the Jeep. "She's solid as a rock."

"Good man!" Seth said, now settled down.

"Look, Seth, I need a favor. I know I'm out here and I have work to do, but something's come up. I haven't taken a vacation in two years. I need a week," Jack asked, totally out of character.

Seth paused at Jack's request. "You need a week? When?"

"Now," Jack said frankly. It was a moment of truth for him. He could lie and say he wanted to breathe mountain air for a while, or, he could play on Seth's understanding Jack knew existed somewhere down in there and just tell him the truth. He took a breath and said, "I met somebody. I'm out here on the road and this morning I met someone that I have to be with for a bit. That's the truth."

There was a pause on the other end of the phone. Seth and Jack had been friends for a few years now and Seth knew Jack had been through a rough breakup from his last relationship. This was really from left field for Jack, but he did say he'd just made a sale.

"You serious? You met someone in a bar? Never go after anyone you meet in a bar, man. It's rule number….something. It never works out." Seth advised.

Jack confessed, "I didn't meet her in a bar. She owns an antique place. I'm telling you, there's something here I haven't felt in a long time. She could be it."

"She could be it? Listen to yourself! Who is this person?"

"Her name is Maggie Styles. She has a place up here called Maggie Styles' Antique Barn. I can't be more honest."

Seth was sitting at his desk and did a search on his computer. "Hang on, I'm Googling her. Here we go." He clicked on her website and her picture came up. "Holy shit! Is this her? Maggie Styles? Dark hair, great rack?"

Jack had to laugh. "That's her. I gotta explore this, man. We both felt something when we met."

Seth was both sympathetic to his friend and protective at the same time. He didn't want to see Jack make a bad call. "You sure about this?"

"Yeah." Then Jack's phone began to beep. "My phone is dying. I gotta go. I didn't charge it last night."

"OK. You've got a week. Be careful out there. I'll call Vail and fix it."

"Seth, I owe you. I'll be in touch."

When Jack hung up, Seth read as much information on Maggie as there was on the site. She was gorgeous, obviously smart and a great catch. Still, for Jack to fall so suddenly was out of character for him. He pushed the intercom button and said, "Paris, come in here, will you?"

Paris came in and Seth said, "Come here. Look at this."

Paris walked around to Seth's computer screen. "Jack just told me he wants a week off to be with this woman."

"What?" Paris was as surprised as Seth was.

"Yeah, tell me about it. He said he met her this morning at this antique place in Colorado. She's hot. I can see the attraction, but Jack doesn't take vacations. He called me and wants a week off to be with her."

Paris studied the picture. "That doesn't sound like Jack. This is weird."

"Look, I know you're a computer geek, and I can't ask you to do anything that's not related to the business, but I need to know about this woman. See what you can dig up on her, will you? Something's not right here. Bring what you find to me. Don't tell Jack yet."

"I'm on it!" Paris wrote Maggie's name down and left. Seth was looking at her picture with an uneasy stare.

Seth wasn't kidding when he said Paris was good with computers. She was really good and one of the best in her field in the little town of Ellijay. She had done Holiday Cabins' website and Seth offered her a job. She liked the mountains and took it. Besides, she could be a contracted hacker from anywhere and her job at Holiday Cabins helped her hide.

Later that afternoon, Jack and Maggie were headed south to meet with Maggie's father. Oddly, even though they had only known each other since morning, there was an air of camaraderie that each secretly welcomed. Jack had spent a lot of time on the road alone and Maggie was about to pull her hair out if she didn't take some time and get off that mountain. Sometimes life presents its own antidotes.

"Tell me about your dad. Was he always into antiques….and pigeons?" Jack took the opportunity to ask.

"Dad is a complicated man. He's obsessive about things. He'll find some antique something at an auction or a sale and totally obsess over getting it. It's a little odd, really, but when he goes after something he doesn't stop until he has it. Then, he shelves it and looks for something else. That barn you were in this morning is a testament to one man's obsession over getting what he wants, even if it does mostly resemble a barn full of junk."

Jack smiled as a profile of her dad was beginning to emerge. "I have a friend like that. He'll find some old car, motorcycle or piece of musical gear that has his name on it and he's gone. It's all he talks about until he finally has it in his garage, and then he doesn't do anything with it except claim it. He'll keep it forever just to say it's his."

"Yep. That's Dad. Hell bent on acquiring his life one piece at a time," Maggie agreed.

"Where did he meet his girlfriend?" Jack asked.

"That's a crazy story," Maggie started.

"Somehow I don't doubt that at all." Jack sighed as he leaned back in his car seat.

"You're going to laugh because it's too textbook."

"Too textbook? Wait a minute, let me guess, they met at a Grateful Dead concert?"

Maggie busted out laughing. "No, not that textbook. He met Lovey at the Grizz. Lovey is Grace's half-sister. She also raises carrier pigeons and he went to buy some. They just fell into each other. Lovey was alone and he was just... interesting to her, I guess. She was a big motivator in his move to Florida. That's where she wanted to be. Far away from here. Besides, like I said, he'd grown tired of the Colorado winters."

"Why did she want to be far away from Grace? Is that family shit only they know?"

"I guess. I didn't ask. I didn't see a lot of Dad for a few years. We give each other space, that's why we get along."

"Lovey? Her name is Lovey?"

Maggie laughed again at Jack's expression. "Yeah, Lovey. That's what we call her. You see, she and Dad smoke a lot of pot. One afternoon they got stoned and watched Gilligan's Island. Thurston Howell's wife is named Lovey on the show, and Dad's girlfriend got up and started doing this great impression of her. I've seen her do it. It's a howl! She's dead on. Anyway, Dad lost it. He laughed for like an hour, and he's called her 'Lovey' ever since. I think it's adorable."

"What have I gotten myself into?" Jack said with his hand on his forehead.

"What happened to your real mother? Is she still alive?" Jack finally addressed the elephant in the conversation. He didn't want to pry, but with all the talk about her father, Maggie never mentioned her mother once. This seemed like an appropriate time.

"Mom died when I was in high school. That's when Dad really started collecting, you know? It gave him something to do besides thinking about her. She was the love of his life. When she went, a part of him went with her. We both had a hard time with it. His pot use really kicked up a notch or two around then as well."

"Was she sick?" Jack asked as he tiptoed around the subject.

"Nah, that was the hell of it. She had gone to the store to get something for dinner. She got broadsided by a guy I went to school with who'd just gotten a new Mustang that morning. I knew him. He was a stoner, so he was probably high as a kite out driving his new car and ran a light. There was never any conclusive evidence to him being all stoned, but I knew him, he was always stoned."

There was a pissed off cynicism in Maggie's voice. Jack could tell she still harbored feelings about that night but was keeping them way down deep in her heart in a place seldom visited. He didn't want to trespass there, but he had to know. "What happened to him? Did he get charged?"

Maggie glanced over at Jack and coldly replied, "Ask God. He died there with Mom. No seatbelt. A regular James Dean. Too cool for school." Jack felt a shiver come over him as he saw a side of Maggie he hadn't expected. He knew people, and Maggie was someone with many layers to her. This fascinated him more and more as the miles rolled away.

Chapter 5

PROPTY OF DANIEL THEODORE BLANCH

As the dust settled from their previous conversation, Maggie stretched in her seat. "Ok, let's see what our 1802 author has to say. Ever use books on tape when you travel?"

"Sometimes, not much. I got 'An Interview with A Vampire' for a present once. I enjoyed that, but I don't listen to them a lot. Why?"

Maggie reached around to the back seat, got the big clasped book, and said," You're about to hear one." She opened the book to the back where the writing was and began to read:

> *"Thes here drawins are the propty of Daniel Theodore Blanch. I am him. I drawed thes tools and hav made them. They work like they should. I will mak mor of thes if someone wants one. I am a good Christan man and I dont want coins or stock fer them. God wanted me to mak them and they are for the good world God made."*

Maggie looked at Jack and laughed. "Oh, hell yeah! These here tools is good!" And they both laughed out loud.

"Keep reading!" Jack said with enthusiasm. "This should be good."

Maggie collected herself and continued reading:

*"Here are what thes tools are and what they is
fer. The first one is a cros saw. It has a ronded
blad other than one long. A man turns the whel
with his feet and the whel cuts the wood."*

Maggie laughed "Ronded blad. That's great!"

Jack looked puzzled. "Round blade operated with his feet? He's talking about a table saw that works like a bicycle does. You pedal the bike and it turns the blade."

"Yeah, so?" Maggie said looking at the picture.

"So, when were the first bicycles invented? That book says 1802, but it was probably finished in 1802, not started in 1802. When were the first bicycles invented?" Jack asked Maggie, who was now impressed with his observation.

"Hell, I don't know. I'm a history professor, as in history of the world, not transportation of it. I'll look it up." Maggie took out her cell phone and googled the question at hand. "It says 1885. The first bike was made in 1885."

"See? Don't you find it odd that this guy knew about pedal and sprocket power almost a hundred years earlier?" Jack asked.

"Chain-driven things have been around for centuries, Jack. Still, I see your point. This guy must have been a visionary as well. He seems like a savant. You know, an illiterate genius? There's more here. Let's read the rest tomorrow."

"My boss is going to have a fit when I give him this," Jack said, shaking his head. Then he and Maggie got quiet. That was the plan all along, to give the book of old tool construction to his boss, but now it seemed they had grown attached to it. Somehow, they had happened upon a little piece of history that seemed as though it was written for them and them alone. It was almost a crime now to give it away. They looked at each other and Maggie said, "I don't see you giving this to anyone."

Jack knew she was right. That look she gave was more than just a knowing glance. Jack almost ran off the road before their gaze broke. It was then he took a leap. He reached out and took her hand and she accepted it like it was meant to be there all along. He nestled back in his seat and felt his heart flutter like a schoolboy. He'd gone out to do his job and had returned with a leading lady for his routine one-act days. Wherever this was going, he was in, and so was Maggie.

"We're not going to make it all the way to Florida, you know. We need to stop somewhere, get some chow, and crash. We can make Florida by tomorrow night," Jack said, as he played the knowing traveler who'd done this route many times before.

"How about a steak?" Maggie began. "I know a place outside Little Rock. There is a Marriott behind it."

"I can do a steak. I'm glad you're not a vegetarian."

Maggie paused and looked at Jack, and how her hand fit so perfectly in his. She hadn't felt like this towards a man in a long time. She had people in her past that, at the moment, seemed to haunt her. That's when she, herself, decided to take a leap.

"No, I'm not a vegetarian, but I am sometimes a vagitarian. Does that bother you?"

Jack felt his heart skip a beat. A *vagitarian*? Did she just tell him she was into girls? He could feel his face begin to blush as he quietly stared at the road ahead. It had been a secret fantasy of his to try a three-way with two girls. He had never pursued it fearing it would wreck the relationship he was in at the time. So, in order to get out of sudden uncomfortable silence that had swept through the SUV, he blurted out "Great! It's good that you aren't held back by what society has deemed proper or improper." He then wished he hadn't said that. "That was a bad thing to say wasn't it?" he said as he grimaced in the wake of his own sudden outburst of taxed morality. "I mean, it's good that you…. shit, I don't know what I mean. What I mean is it's okay. It doesn't bother me. I think. Why would it?"

Maggie sat watching him back himself into a corner. It was becoming apparent they were in the dawning stages of a relationship and certain things had to break the surface for it to work. "Have you ever been with two women at once, Jack Reynolds, seller of fine prefabricated cabins from Ellijay, Georgia?"

Jack hated the fact he was so green when it came to "wild sex," but the truth was, he was. All his relationships up to now had been long term. Four years, five years and then eleven years with few one night stands in between. Then it dawned on him that maybe that's why they never lasted. Maybe he was too boring. "No, I haven't, Maggie Styles owner of Maggie Style's Antique Barn on Maggie Mountain in Colorado. I have lived a sheltered life."

"Ever wanted to?" Maggie said in a matter of fact tone.

"Sure! What guy hasn't? I just never had the…um…"

"Balls?" Maggie interrupted.

Jack looked at her and laughed. "Yeah, I just never had the balls."

Maggie studied the face of the man fate had dealt her. He was cute as hell, in good shape, smart and had a great sense of humor. How had he not ended up with a pair of party girls she couldn't figure. The one thing she did know was that she liked him more and more by the minute.

"If it bothers you Jack, I understand. I mean, if it threatens you."

"We are there aren't we?" Jack said in a soft tone, trying to ease into the moment.

"Where are we, Jack? Are we someplace that you didn't count on just like I didn't? You walked into my life this morning and I feel like I've known you forever. Everything you say is exactly what I want to hear. The way you smile at me, the way you know things that you're not supposed to. Your……you-ness!"

"My…..me-ness?" Jack looked at Maggie and their hands together. His eyes met hers as the lines of the road reflected in both their eyes.

"There is something I need to know, Maggie."

"Go for it," Maggie said as she braced herself for what request was to come.

Jack leaned in and said, "What's the name of that restaurant? We're almost to Little Rock."

Maggie remained frozen and said, "Two exits up. Olin's Steakhouse behind the Marriott. Don't eat too much."

"Why not?" Jack whispered.

Maggie leaned back in her seat still looking at him. She smiled and said, "Because I'm going to fuck your brains out when we get to that damn Marriott."

Chapter 6

THE LAST THREE PAGES

The next morning Jack and Maggie were exhausted from marathon sex all night, now, they were on their way to see her father. Maggie leaned back in her seat as the second half of their trip began. She smiled and looked over at Jack, who overnight had become the only man she wanted.

"How did you do that? I never thought I'd fall for a man named 'Jack.' I always thought it would be someone with a kingly name like 'Napoleon Rothschild' or a man on a white horse with a mask like Zorro who climbs into my room through my window and takes my virtue under a full moon."

Jack laughed and went into his Clark Gable voice with, "Honey, I hate to tell you, but I do believe your virtue was taken a long time ago and Zorro rode a black horse, not a white one."

"Ahhh! Are you coloring me a harlot?" Maggie asked in a mocked Southern tone.

"If you are a harlot madam, you're best harlot I've ever seen," Jack answered with a wink.

"Well, at least I know I'm appreciated." Maggie almost blushed.

Jack laughed and replied, "Honey, if I were any more appreciative, we'd still be back in that motel room."

Maggie smiled and sat back like a child, totally content in playing in her dirty clothes. She was so beautiful to Jack it made him catch his breath. He began to remember her, as she stood in front of him just hours before, slowly unbuttoning her shirt, revealing nothing underneath but pure woman. She took his hands in hers and placed them inside her shirt and then moved to him. His hands ran up her bare back as their mouths connected in a life-altering kiss. It was deep, sensual and animalistic. She unbuckled his belt, unzipped his pants and slid her hand down to feel his hardened appreciation, which was straining against his (soon to be discarded) Fruit of The Looms. It was all playing out again in his mind when he caught himself getting yet another erection.

"Shit!" Jack said as he caught himself.

Maggie looked over at him and softly laughed. "Yeah, shit." She, too, was back in the room, feeling him take her like they'd done it many times before.

"Going to be a long drive. Want to hear more from Mister Blanch? I gotta do something or I'm going to have my hand in my pants in about a minute." She looked down at his obvious predicament and coaxed, "Easy cowboy. We don't want to wear out your toolbox."

Reaching around to get the ledger they had begun reading the day before, Maggie said, "Let's see, when we last left Mister Blanch, he'd just made a drill bit." They both laughed at the absurdity of it. "I'm going to skip all the tools crap and go to the last pages. There's like actual stuff written there. Funny, the ink looks different. Here we go…. this time there's a date." Maggie began to read.

> *"Springtim, 1785. It is a good day today. Im gona try to see Elizbeth Kortright at the stor when I by flar. I love her derly. She will come home here and be with me and not go back to New York wher she cam from. I wil tel her today that I want her. It is a good day."*

"Oh, Jack, he's a romantic. How great. He can't spell for shit, but he's in love."

"I wonder if she knows that," Jack laughed.

"Oh, stop. He's a sweetheart. I can tell."

Maggie continued reading:

> *"I saw Elizbeth today and she wod hardly tawk to me! I love her and she wodnt say mor than a helo to me. Bart Cambel told me she was maring that upity feler from Vergina. Hes not takin her!"*

"Wooo!" Jack groaned. "We got a little soap opera here. He's from Vergina too."

Maggie kept reading to herself for a minute.

"Well? What happened next? Did he kick the guy's ass or what?" Jack asked the silent Maggie.

Suddenly, she sat straight up in her seat and said loudly, "Oh my God! He killed him!"

Jack jumped at her urgency. "He killed who? Who killed what?"

Maggie kept reading with a look on her face that was as close to panic as Jack had known. "Will you tell me what happened?"

Maggie began to read again:

> *"I done went and tok the man who tok my Elizbeth from me and I made him ded. His nam was Jimy Monro. His dobl brother I herd him cal Spenc run off or Ida kilt him to. I kilt Monro with a stob. Now my Elizbeth wil be with me. I hav the notbok he wrot her love leters in I tok from his pokit. My Elizbeth wont nevr see non of them. I hid it here and nobody gon no."*

Jack looked at Maggie from the driver's seat and concluded, "It sounds like that guy is a murderer. He confessed to it. Too bad he's dead or we'd be on Unsolved Mysteries."

Maggie didn't say a word but franticly took out her phone and began typing.

Jack was fascinated. "What is it? You going to call the cops on our boy here? It's a little late for...."

Maggie interrupted him, saying, "Wait a minute. I've got to look something up."

Jack sat looking at her while her eyes strained for her Internet to work faster. "Yes!" she said. "Here we go."

"Where are we going? What's up?" Jack asked, looking at the now totally absorbed Maggie.

"Holy fuck! Pull over. Jack pull over! Stop the car!"

"Damn woman, hang on." Jack began to pull the car over to the side of the road. Maggie looked white as a sheet. "Will you tell me what's up? Did he kill someone else?"

Maggie looked up at Jack and was shaking. "Jack, I did my master's thesis on the impact of The Missouri Compromise. It was over slavery. One of the key figures in the deal was James Monroe. It was his baby. He went on to be President of the United States. It says here that Blanch killed a Jimmy Monroe. 'Jimmy' as in 'James.' People did call him Jimmy sometimes in old texts."

"Oh, come on. How many Jimmy, or James, Monroes can there be from back then? There's no way to tell." Jack offered.

"Yeah, how many Elizabeth Kortrights?" Maggie asked. "I remembered her name from school. I made fun of it sounding like the Cartwrights from Bonanza. Blanch killed Jimmy Monroe who was in love with Elizabeth Kortright. Blanch said his double brother Spence ran off and didn't get killed. I remember reading that James Monroe had a brother named Spence who supposedly died when he was a kid of, like, two years old. Spence was named for his father, who was also named 'Spence'. What if that's a mistake and James Monroe really did have a twin brother who was alive? What if when James was killed by Blanch, Spence Monroe took his brother's place and nobody caught on? It says here that James Monroe married Elizabeth Kortright in 1786. That's a year after Blanch says he killed him. I'm telling you, according to this, if it's true, Spence Monroe took his brother's place, married Elizabeth Kortright, and then went on to be President. Jack, this re-writes history. The pamphlet we have, it was written by James Monroe, and he got into political trouble because of it. That must be why Blanch had it. A souvenir."

"So, you're saying James Monroe had an identical twin that supposedly died as a kid, but turned up in Virginia with James? If this is true, then how did Blanch know which one to kill? They are supposedly identical, right?"

Maggie studied the book and said, "Notebook! Jack, he said he took a notebook from Monroe. That notebook would be in the real James Monroe's handwriting, and if we had it, we could compare the handwriting styles. We'd know if it was the real James Monroe or not. There are samples of James Monroe's handwriting we can access in a museum in Fredericksburg, Virginia. The James Monroe Museum. I've been there."

"This is insane, Maggie. This is some real craziness. So, do we still need to go see your father? You want to drag him into all this? He'll think we've lost our minds. It sounds like he's already pretty close to losing his."

"Dad will know where he got the trunk. We need to know because we still may be able to find the notebook. Don't you see? This is history!"

"Maggie, it was what, two hundred and some odd years ago? That notebook is dust by now, burned up, destroyed. Petrified goat shit. In other words, gone. We don't have a prayer of finding it. What else does the book say?"

Jack began pulling back onto the road as Maggie turned her attention to the book once more.

> *"I got forty three dolers and I can git me and Elizbeth a good hors and cart. I can tak her here to live. I no she lovs me. I wil see her tomoro and I wil tak her wild flowers and tel*

*her that I want her now that I kilt that Monro
feler and put his carcas in the wal behind the
river rocks and mud. She won't never no."*

"Whoa!" Jack let out. "Blanch walled the guy up somewhere. This is wild."
Maggie read the next entry.

*"That Monro felers dobl brother done stold my
Elizbeth! I went to see her today and that man
Spenc that loks just like Monro was kisin her
behin the stor. Im gon kil that man lik I don kilt
that othern then my Elizbeth wil be with me not
him."*

*"They are gone! That Spenc don tok my
Elizbeth off. I was gon kil him but now he is
gon. I wil find him and kil him lik I don kilt his
doble brother."*

*"My Elizbeth is gon from me now. She was al I
loked fer and now I cant see her no mor. Bart
Cambel said they had movd on and he was a
upity politiks man. I got no ned for no politiks
man in my hom here that was fer Elizbeth. Im
gon git me a new woman. I am not never gointo
see my Elizbeth again. I am left with the stinkin
of that Monro feler."*

*It is now Winter of the year of our Lord 1802. It
has been hard. I have not rote in this book fer a
long spel. I am sick. My wif Hope was taken
from me in the Springtime. Pamla, my sweet
dawter and me put the flat rock I chizled fer her
marker face down besid our home near the
waterfall. She liked it ther. The church yard
would not take her. My hands are almost gone*

*now. Im sendin Pamla to liv with Bart Cambel
and his wif. Hope never did nuthin to him. I am
going to see God soon. I will not rit in this bok
no mor.*

Maggie closed the book and ran her hand across the back of it. She looked over at Jack and said, "That's it. That's all there is."

"Oh, man!" Jack said. "He was living with that corpse in his wall. Can you imagine?"

"In his wall?" Maggie said as she had a revelation. "Jack, there are a lot of really old buildings and houses near Fredericksburg. I did a lot of research there when I did my thesis on Monroe. If we can find out where Blanch lived, there is a chance the bones of the real James Monroe are still there."

"What? Man, you are reaching here, darlin'. I mean, looking for love letters is one thing, but looking for a skeleton in a wall, in a place that we have no idea if it even exists, is crazy."

"It's possible. I'm telling you, it's possible. Blanch said he lived near a waterfall. How many of those can there be? We need to get to Dad. He'll know where he got this thing. He'll know if it came from Virginia or not."

"Man, what are the odds of this? I go to Colorado to sell a few cabins and I end up with a woman who's hell-bent on looking for the skeleton of the fifth President of the United States' dead brother who apparently didn't care about him getting killed because he just took over the man's life and stole his woman. It's one hell of a day."

"It is indeed," Maggie said under her breath. "It is indeed."

Chapter 7

IS THAT HAIR?

At around eight o'clock that evening Jack and Maggie made the final turn on their road trip. Sea Gull Lane in Amelia Island, Florida, at last.

"Which one is it?" Jack asked as he looked at the flat, sandy yards along the street.

"You'll know," Maggie said, like she was anticipating a well-planned joke to spring up at any time. Then, it did.

"Oh, my God! You gotta be kiddin' me. This is great. It looks like the set of 'Rowan and Martin's Laugh-In' from the sixties."

"I told you, you'd know," Maggie smirked. "Wow, Dad added more daisies. He loves daisies."

As Jack pulled into the driveway behind the van, he parked the car and just sat looking. He could still see the tie-dyed curtains, the black light lit room with day glow painted posters from the early sixties and seventies. There was a five-foot peace sign that hung out in the yard and around the side of the house he could see cages made of old wood and chicken wire.

"Are those pigeon cages?"

Maggie leaned over and looked down the side of the house and said, "Yep. There's more around the back. Listen….."

"To what?" Jack whispered.

"Shhhhh. Listen to the music."

Jack leaned forward and he could hear the soundtrack to the musical Hair playing in the background. "Is that Hair?"

"I'm impressed! Dad loves it. Plays it all the time."

"I'm speechless. I'm absolutely speechless." Jack said as he just sat in amazement.

Maggie got out and stretched her back as straight as possible. Jack followed as they slowly walked up to the front door and rang the bell. When the door opened, the two were thrown back to 1968 as a short little man resembling a cross between Jerry Garcia and Elmo from Sesame Street met them, totally elated.

"Mags!" he yelled, as he threw his arms around Maggie like he hadn't seen her in forever. "My little baby girl! I didn't know you were coming." He looked at Jack and said, "Who's this? He with you?"

"Yeah, I'm with her," Jack replied as he stood in bewilderment the man hadn't put that together. Jack put out his hand and said, "I'm Jack Reynolds."

"Holy shit! You two married?" the little man asked, as he eyed Jack up and down.

"Maggie and I drove down from Colorado to see you. She told me a lot about you. I love your house, and no, we're not married."

"It's a beaut ain't it? Call me Wood. Everybody does. Glad you're not married. The government watches you when you get married."

"Wood?" Jack questioned as if he'd misheard something.

Maggie had to laugh. "I'll tell you the story later."

She turned to Wood and asked, "Can we come in? I gotta pee."

"Hell yeah! Come on in here." Wood motioned for the two to come into the house.

It was truly like Jack and Maggie had just stepped out of a time capsule. As they walked into the living room, the odor of marijuana hit them like a wave. Jack looked at Maggie and did a mocking gesture like he was smoking a joint. Maggie looked at him and just shrugged. The house was filled with lava lamps of every color of the rainbow; plants were on every table and in every corner. As Maggie disappeared into the bathroom Jack was left alone with this most interesting little man.

"How long you and Mags been shacked up? She's a great gal, even if she is my own kid. Hey, you want to do a bong hit? It's primo!"

"Maybe later," Jack said as he tried to wrap his head around all that was happening. "Right now, I'm just glad to be somewhere other than the road."

"I hear ya. I spent my share of time out there when I was collecting for the Barn. Hey, you go see Maggie's Barn?" Wood asked.

"Yeah. That's where we met. I was looking for some old tools and we just….."

Maggie walked in and before Jack could finish said, "Dad, you bothering Jack? Go easy on him will you? I don't want you to run him off." As she leaned up against the wide-eyed Jack, she said, "Did you say something about a bong hit?"

"That's my girl!" Wood said as he headed for the couch and coffee table.

Jack and Maggie followed to the soundtrack of Hair. Jack turned to Maggie and whispered, "The music is great."

"Where's Lovey? She not here?" Maggie inquired as she tiptoed around the living room.

"She's in the bedroom. She has a client. Nice guy but I think he's a fairy. Don't tell Lovey I said that. She'll get all in my face about stereotypes. Shit like that."

Jack's eyebrows went way up. Client? Bedroom? Naturally he thought what anyone would when you put those two words together.

Maggie accepted the bong her dad had just prepared for her and took her first deep hit. Jack watched as Wood held the lighter over the bowl and the bubbles brought the cylinder to life as it filled with white smoke. Wood took his finger off the carburetor hole on the tube, exhausting all the smoke into Maggie's lungs and said, "Boom! That's a good one."

Maggie fell back into the pillows on the couch holding it in as long as possible. As she exhaled, the smoke came out like an avalanche running down a mountainside. As Maggie got her breath back, she tapped her chest in approval. "Where'd you get that? That's nice."

"One of Lovey's people. He didn't have any dough to pay her so he gave her some of the weed he grew. I'm tellin' you, the guy may be screwed up in the head, but he sure can grow pot."

The weed hit Maggie pretty quickly. She looked at Jack sitting there with his mouth hanging open while Wood talked about his wife's clients in the bedroom and got his daughter stoned. She busted out laughing and put her face in her hand. She looked up at Jack and said, "Jack, Lovey is a hypnotist. She helps people through hypnosis. It's a kind of therapy. Things people can't do themselves. She takes them deep into their subconscious and they figure out things like why they can't stop smoking, why they hate their mothers or whatever issues they have. She's quite good at it. She's also clairvoyant. She can read people like nobody I've ever seen. When she gets a vibe on something or someone, look out. She's dangerous." Then she looked at Wood and said, "Dad load him a bowl then it'll all make sense." She started laughing again and Wood joined in. Now Jack felt totally out of place. He hadn't gotten stoned in a long time, but something told him he was about to.

"Screw it. Load that sucker," Jack declared, nodding to the still smoldering bong.

"I like this guy, Mags. He's got potential," Wood said, as he pinched some fine green powder off a little tray.

Wood handed Jack the bong and five minutes later Jack looked like a cat on a spinning washing machine.

"I told you this was rockin' weed," Wood laughed, as he held open the baggy with the last of the pot in it. "Take a whiff." He extended it to Jack and Maggie who gestured with a 'thumbs up' hand signal. "So, what brings you to Florida? Don't say you were just in the neighborhood."

"Oh, shit," Jack said with a free-falling look. "The ledger! We gotta show him the…"

Just then the door to the back bedroom flew open and Indian chanting music could be heard mingling with the sixties sound track already in the air. Jack and Maggie jumped and turned to see a woman at least six feet, two inches tall with long brick red hair come spinning down the hallway.

"Oh Wooooooody! Woooooooody!? Are you out here?"

Wood called back, "Lovey Dooooooevey! Guess who's heeeeeere?"

Lovey entered the room to see Maggie and Jack. "Mags!" she yelled as she flung herself at Maggie, knocking them both to the floor.

"When did you get here? Oh, my God! I missed you soooo much!"

Lovey hugged and kissed on Maggie like a Labrador just in from the kennel. "It's been soooo long!"

Jack was a stoned mess, sitting in an armchair, starry-eyed and not missing a thing. This huge, gyrating brick-topped woman had Maggie on the floor not letting her up and he couldn't move. Lovey finally got up and turned to look at Jack and said, "Hey you handsome thing. I'm Lovey."

"Where on earth had they landed?" was all Jack kept thinking. He'd heard of weird in-laws, but this was a story from the depths of crazy. A brick-top Amazon woman and a little man who's lost in the sixties, no contact with the world outside other than pigeons and hearsay from those he did see. He looked at Maggie, bent his head down and started to laugh uncontrollably.

"I like him," Lovey said. "He's happy!"

"He's baked," Maggie said with a sympathetic smile.

Lovey looked at Maggie and asked, "Where did you find him?"

She looked up in her stoned state and loudly blurted out, "He sells prefabricated cabins from Georgia!" Jack, already in hysterics, opened his mouth as wide as it would go. He rolled over onto the floor, held his stomach and laughed as hard as anyone had ever laughed at anything. Maggie fell on top of him and they both held onto each other until the wave of absurdity subsided enough that they each took a breath.

Wood and Lovey just watched them until Wood at last said in his little voice, "So, anybody want a candy apple?" Maggie and Jack were gone again.

When Jack and Maggie at last got up off the floor and had settled into their seats, they heard a man's voice say, "Thank you, Mistress. I'll call you soon." They turned to see a huge man of at least four hundred pounds waddle through the living room, take a cowboy hat off a hat rack and walk out the door. Jack looked at Maggie and said, "What next?" He was still in spasms from moments before when the tornado of laughter swept through the room.

"That's Little Stevie Caldwell. He has issues." Lovey said as she watched the headlights head down the flat Florida street.

"I'll say!" Jack agreed. "Who wears cowboy hats in Florida? Are you helping him to stop eating so much? Somewhere there's a horse that'll thank you for it."

"No, he can't stop sleeping in cat litter. He can't sleep 'less he's all wallowed up in it. He's got an eight-foot cat box in his bedroom." Lovey revealed with a shrug.

Jack fell into a soft laughter and just shook his head.

"Well, you asked what was next," Maggie said, trying to hold in her own outburst.

Maggie collected herself as much as she could and looked at Wood with what little degree of seriousness she could muster. "Dad, we found something at the Barn, and I need to know where it came from. It's an old trunk that looks kind of like an old pirate treasure chest. It's about this big and this wide," she said as she mocked the height and width with her hands. "It was full of old books from somewhere. We found some really important stuff in there, and we need to know where it came from. Do you remember at all where you got it?"

"Old trunk? You mean the one on top of the saw?" Wood asked.

Jack, still quite stoned, yelled out, "Yes! Bingo. I can't believe in all that mess out there you remembered it was sitting on top of a saw. An old two-man hand saw, right?"

"Yeah, that's it." Wood began. "I remembered it because I didn't want to sell the saw. I needed it for something and I slid the trunk on top of it to remind myself not to sell it."

"What did you need it for?" Maggie asked.

"Beats me. I needed it for something, though."

"Dad, it's really important that we find out where that trunk came from. Do you remember where you got it?"

"Sure, I know exactly where I got it. It was my dad's. It came from his house when he died. That's where I got the saw, now that I think about it."

Jack and Maggie looked at each other with a puzzled grin. "You got the trunk from Grandpa? Where did he get it?"

"Hell, he said it was a family heirloom. Said he'd had it for years, passed down from his dad. Why? I forgot about it. I guess if it's being passed down it's your baby now. Congratulations! It's a trunk!" Wood said as he slapped his knee and busted out laughing.

Maggie leaned into Wood and said, "Dad, do you know what's in the trunk? Did you ever open it?"

Wood scratched his head. "Can't say I did. Never figured out how, without breaking the binding that is. Only an idiot would tear up an old piece like that trying to get it open."

Jack felt an "oh, shit!" moment come over him as he remembered taking the crowbar and opening the trunk.

"How'd you get it open?" Wood asked Maggie.

"Jack is really good at getting into tight places. He has a special key and we used that." She winked at Jack, who seemed obviously relieved.

"Well, look at you. You're full of surprises," Wood said

as his approval rating of Jack just went up. "What's in it? I been luggin' that sucker around for years. I figured I'd open it one day. Never did. What'd you find?"

"We found some really old books," Maggie said, as she began her explanation of the ledger.

"Oh, I love old books!" Lovey yelled out. "I read them to my clients sometimes. I read *Gone with The Wind* to a client once. The whole thing. He was paying by the hour so what the hell?"

"Why did he want you to read that?" Jack asked.

"He thought the book was about him in another life. He wanted to go back in a regression and see if he had done any of the stuff Scarlett did."

"Scarlett?" Jack said in a puzzled tone. "Why not Rhett Butler?"

"Because he didn't think he was Rhett Butler, he thought he was Scarlett O'Hara. I read the whole book to him trying to let him decide whether or not he really was her."

"But Scarlett didn't exist." Jack commented.

"She didn't exist that we know. Why did Margaret Mitchell write it? Think about it. A lone little woman in Atlanta wrote one of the biggest literary legacies of our time. Just like that? Had to be more going on there. Past life regressions can take us places we never thought of. I have helped hundreds over the years go back and make things right. In their own minds anyway."

"She's the real deal," Wood said with confidence. "I've seen her make a grown man cry like a baby. It's crazy shit, but hey, it got us this weed, so what the hell? What kinds of books were in the trunk?"

Maggie motioned with her head for Jack to go out to the car and get Blanch's journal. "We found several really old books from the late 1700's and early 1800's. One was really special, Dad. James Monroe, President James Monroe, wrote it before he became President. I think it's worth a fortune."

"No kiddin'?" Wood exclaimed. "I've been movin' that thing around for years and you tell me there was actually something in there worth something?"

"Well, yeah. I think it may be a real historic find. And you say it was handed down to you from my grandfather? I have to know where he got it."

"Why? What difference does it make where they got it as long as you have it now?"

Lovey chimed in. "I don't think any of your dead family will object, darlin'."

Jack returned with the ledger. He handed it to Maggie and she explained, "This is why. This is a ledger from a man in 1802. He made tools and chronicled them here, see?" Maggie opened the book to show Wood and Lovey the illustrations. "This guy, Daniel Blanch, describes them in detail. Then, here in the back, he talks about a man who was in love with the same woman he was. Blanch killed the man and put him behind a wall in a building in Fredericksburg, Virginia. Dad, we think the man who was killed was the real James Monroe. The James Monroe that became President in 1817 was really his twin brother, Spence Monroe, who history reports as dying at around age two. We think Blanch killed James, put him in a wall somewhere in Virginia, and then Spence Monroe took over his brother's life. He then went on to be President."

Wood looked at Lovey, then back at Jack and Maggie. Jack was coming back to a state of reality and said, "She's not kiddin', man. We read it coming down here. There is a good chance that we've stumbled onto a piece of history never supposed to be seen by anyone. Now, we need to find out who Daniel Blanch was and where he came from."

"You sayin' all that was in that old trunk? Man! That's some real Hardy Boys shit right there. I don't know anything about James Monroe, but Daniel Blanch won't be that hard to find out about."

"Why do you say that?" Maggie asked, surprised at Wood's response.

"Because he was your, let's see, great, great, great, great, great......great grandfather."

Jack and Maggie look at each other as both really straightened up. "What?" They both yelled at once. "Are you saying Daniel Blanch was related to me? A man who killed a President. Or almost President? Or something?"

"Yeah," Wood confirmed. "I have a family tree book somewhere and I remember him bein' one of the first branches on it. I made a joke about the whole 'Blanch-branch' of the tree. It doesn't go back much further than that. I'll find it for you tomorrow if you like."

"Dad, I have to see that. Where is it? Can we get it now?"

"It's in the garage," Wood said, as he reached for another pinch of weed on the tray in front of him.

"Oh, for Pete's sake," Lovey blurted out. "If it's in the garage then you better wait. It's full. You couldn't get another pencil in there. I've been after him to go through that junk, but he won't. Says it's valuable."

Maggie looked at Wood and asked, "You been collecting again?"

"Yeah. You know me. It's in my blood. Just like you. I got some good stuff out there, too. You might want to get a truck and take some of it back to the Barn with you."

Jack remembered the Barn. "I don't think you could get another pencil in that barn of hers either. It's pretty loaded."

"Dad, do you remember anything at all about Blanch? Here, look at this. Does it mean anything to you at all?"

Maggie laid the ledger down in Wood's lap. He opened it and studied the illustrations, gently turning the pages. He seemed to be remembering something he wasn't saying. Maggie was picking up on it and asked him, "Dad, are you sure you've never seen this before?"

"Wow. This was in that old trunk? Wish I'd known that. This is great! No wonder Dad told me to hang onto it. And no, I've never seen this before. Why you askin'?"

Lovey seemed agitated. The three looked at her when she made a slight earthy grunting noise. "Let me see that."

Wood laid the ledger on her lap and she let her hands rub across it, then suddenly jumped back, startled. Lovey pushed the ledger off her lap like it was a huge insect and got up and stood away from it.

"What on earth?" Jack exclaimed as he looked at Lovey staring at the ledger on the floor.

"Get that thing out of here!" She yelled. "Get it out!" It's evil! It wants something. That thing has no purpose here. Take it outside. I don't want it here."

Maggie stood up to comfort her and Lovey stepped back. "Why did you bring that here? It needs to be locked away in that trunk where you got it. It's fucking evil, I'm telling you!"

"Lovey it's just an old book. I found something in it we needed to talk to Dad about and….."

"Mags, I love you like my own daughter but if you are going to keep that book with you, I have to ask you to leave. That thing has an energy around it like I've never felt. It has its own heartbeat. You know what that means? It means that it has a soul. A soul dark and evil. Get it out of here."

"What if I put it back in the car?" Jack asked Lovey. "I don't want anyone upset here."

"Fine," Lovey said, still staring at the ledger. "You put it back in the car and park the car down the street. I don't want it anywhere near me or this house."

Jack looked at Maggie. She motioned with her head for Jack to take the book out to the car. When he was outside, Maggie said, "It's gone now, darlin'. It's cool. It's outside."

"What the hell, Love?" Wood began. "I've never seen you do that before."

Lovey looked at Maggie and repeated, "Mags you gotta get rid of that thing. It's evil! I'm telling you, there is a dark force around that book. You say you got it in a trunk? An old trunk?"

"Yeah. It's really old and beat up." Jack said cautiously.

"Describe it to me in detail. What did it look like? Did it have any crosses or angels or any religious markings at all on it?"

"No. Not that I saw," as Maggie tried to remember the old trunk in detail. "Dad, you had it longer than I did. What do you remember about it?"

"It was heavy! It was heavy and dirty. That's about it.

Dad gave me the trunk and the saw, maybe some other stuff, but I don't remember exactly. Like I said, I never opened the trunk."

Maggie was becoming frustrated. "What other stuff? Was there something else with it? Think! I've gotta know. This is important."

Wood seemed like he was trying to remember a face in a crowd.

She turned to Jack and said, "We've gotta know if there is anything else out there. There could be something to do with the Monroe murder. We've got to go see as soon as we can."

"Maggie, I'm not just getting in the car tomorrow and driving back to Colorado. All this is exciting and weird, yeah, but the reality of it is a long shot at best and you know it."

Jack had a point. He had driven her this far, and now she was beckoning him to follow her further into this two hundred year old mystery. It had suddenly gone from a minor curiosity to a major one, with a more sinister vibe around it. She couldn't ask him to do more. Maggie knew how they felt about each other, but something was pushing her down a road where she couldn't ask him to go.

Reaching for Jack's hand, she said, "Look, let's turn in and talk about this in the morning. You're right. We're tired and I'm as stoned as you are. Let's just go to bed and when we wake up in the morning it'll all be clear as a bell."

He looked at the woman he'd fallen for so deeply and had to give in. When he stood up, Maggie turned to Wood and said, "We're gone. Is my room clean by chance, or have you put stuff in there as well as the garage?"

"It's clean." Lovey assured her. "I keep it in case a client sleeps over." She looked at Maggie and winked.

Jack went out to get their suitcases and Maggie got a second to talk to Lovey. "I trust you. You know that you crazy old witch. But I gotta know, how much of all that was true about the ledger and how much was you just bein' freaky?"

"Mags, there is something around that ledger. It's dark.

I'm tellin' you. Stay as far away from all this as you can. Take it back to Colorado, put it back in the trunk and burn it all. Nothing but bad will come of what you find. Let it all go, darlin'. This is some powerful shit. Let it go."

"I found all this for a reason. I know I did. What are the odds I would do my research on the very thing that James Monroe was famous for? Its all a crazy set of circumstances. I have to find out more about it. It's just too weird."

Lovey was looking at Jack through the window getting the suitcases. "What's his story? You known him long?"

"I met him yesterday. He's part of all this somehow, I know it. When I met him we were drawn together. He felt it just like I did."

"I felt drawn to him too, but I'm a horny old bitch," Lovey admitted. "You bang him yet?"

"Damn woman, you ARE a horny old bitch. We stayed outside Little Rock last night in that Marriott behind Olin's."

"Little Rock, huh? Did you get his little rocks off?" Lovey continued as she inspected Jack's ass hanging out from behind the car.

"Stop! And yeah, he's awesome in the sack. Just remember, he's mine, you old horn dog."

Maggie gave Lovey a sisterly hug. "I'll be careful, but I gotta play this out."

Jack came in with the suitcases and Lovey showed him the bedroom. Soon, Jack and Maggie were in bed staring at the ceiling. They could still hear the stereo out in the other room, which had now switched to The Who's 'Tommy.' "Man, this is messed up. I never counted on any of this. Yesterday, we found a ledger. Now we're back in the sixties in Florida. What a trip! That was crazy great pot. I haven't been that stoned since..... I was that stoned. Hell, I'm still buzzed. One bong hit!"

"You did great out there," Maggie said (like she was giving him a review of a game). "They like you. Dad likes you a lot."

"Your dad is a nut! What a character. Wood. Where did he get that name, by the way?"

Maggie started to giggle. "It had to be thirty years ago. Dad went to one of his friend's funeral with five other guys. They were always together doing crazy shit. Well, after the funeral, they got stoned and Dad changed out of his suit, back into his blue jeans and tie-dyed shirt with sandals. The rest of the guys stayed in their suits for the trip home, for some reason. On the way, they were all in a van and got pulled over by a cop who was a real asshole, apparently. He made them all get out of the van and line up. He looked at Dad, with his long hair and sixties clothes, and said, "Hey Woodstock, you stand by the car. You holding?" The rest of the guys busted out laughing and they started calling him 'Woodstock' from then on. Somewhere along the way, it got shortened to just 'Wood'. Now you know. You also know that we need to get back to Colorado to see what's around the trunk, if anything, then go to Fredericksburg to find James Monroe."

"Damn it Maggie! I told you I have to get back to Ellijay. I have been off the grid here for way too long. I'm surprised helicopters aren't flying around now looking for my ass. I can't go. Why don't you go and I'll go back to the plant and see if I have a job or not."

"I told you I'd buy a cabin from you. I meant that. When I sell that book in the safe deposit box I'll be loaded. How many cabins were you going to sell in Colorado? Remember that conversation? We are on a mission, Jack. You're the reason we are in this. It's all because of you. It's history we are dealing with here. It's exciting!"

"That's another thing. Did you ever stop to think that maybe, just maybe, there are people out there that like history the way it is? You're fooling with a Presidential legacy here. People who mess with things like this have a tendency to disappear, never to be seen again. I don't want to disappear for you, James Monroe, or anyone. We have to walk softly on this, or we could end up in a wall of our own somewhere. Besides, it's a long way to Colorado and I just made that trip. I've no desire to do it again any time soon."

"We'll fly back." Maggie suggested. "I'll pay for it. We can be on a plane by tomorrow afternoon. We'll fly into Denver, and then rent a car back to The Barn. This time tomorrow, we'll be back in Colorado. No problem."

Jack let out a moment of silence. Maggie was next to him with a fire in her that was hypnotic. Her passion was contagious. She wanted something so outside his usual train of thinking that he almost knew he would go before she asked him to. Not to go seemed more of a crime against humanity. After all, how many times in your life do you get to derail a President's legacy? And if you could, why would you want to? It was going to be a long night.

After his pause, Jack finally said, "I don't fly United. They wrecked a guy's guitar and wouldn't fix it. It was viral video on YouTube. That's just wrong."

Maggie smiled and gave an elated "So you'll go?"

Jack let out a deep sigh and said, "Yeah, I'll go." Then he rolled over, looked at Maggie and said, "So, Wood is short for Woodstock. That makes perfect sense. Finally, something about this place that makes sense. All of you have little nicknames and I'm just plain ol' Jack."

"You want a nickname? Be careful what you wish for. You may get it," Maggie warned as she rolled over to face Jack. "You know what? I lost something."

"What'd you lose?" Jack asked, looking back at her.

Maggie began to play with the hair on Jack's chest.

"I'm not sure but I think I might know where it is."

Curious, Jack asked, "What are you saying, you nutty professor?"

"Nutty professor, huh? Well, let's see if I can find that damned thing. I know it's here somewhere. Wait. I think it's under the covers. I'll be right back. I'm going to check."

As Maggie disappeared under the covers, Jack watched

as her head slowly made its way further and further down until he could hear a muffled, "There it is!" come from down below. Jacked gasped and closed his eyes as Maggie took care of her impulse to take him into her mouth and keep him there for the duration of his rapidly approaching erection, which was already well on its way to being a fond memory.

Chapter 8

I WAS THERE!

The next morning, Jack and Maggie woke up to the sound of "Crimson and Clover," by Tommy James and the Shondells.

Jack was trying to wake up. "You gotta be kidding me. It wasn't a dream. I'm in a sixties movie!"

Maggie rolled over and groaned, "Sounds like Dad's up. Tommy James. I wish I had a dollar for every time I've heard that song."

Wood and Lovey were already well into their day. As Jack and Maggie walked out into the living room, Wood appeared wearing a Beatles cooking apron. Lovey, wearing a pair of black tights, was on the floor doing what looked like some form of Yoga. Her tall frame made her look more like a big black pretzel. "Morning!" Wood exclaimed. "Breakfast is served."

All Jack could say was, "Coffee."

"Coffee we got. We got a feast to go with it. There's a bowl loaded for ya in the bong. Go for it! It's morning."

Jack looked at Maggie and said, "Wake and bake? Man, I haven't done that since college. I gotta pass." Maggie nodded and they turned the corner to the kitchen. A feast of waffles, eggs, bacon, sausage, fruit, toast and a stack of pancakes Aunt Jemima would deem worthy awaited them. "Holy shit! Look at all this," Maggie said. "Dad, you went overboard."

Jack and Maggie sat down and ate as much as possible,

trying not to hurt Wood's feelings. Lovey appeared to be in a meditative state in the floor oblivious to everything going on around her.

Jack whispered, "How long has she been there?" as he looked around the corner at Lovey.

Wood just shrugged. "Got me. She was like that when I got up. When she says she needs to go within, I stay out of it."

Maggie then got serious.

"Dad, we have to go back to the Barn today because I've got to look further into whatever this thing is with the ledger. We're flying back this afternoon."

Wood led Maggie to the doorway where a suitcase sat in front of it. "We're goin' with you to the Barn. Surprise!"

"What? Dad, no. I can't drag you into this. There is no telling where it will take us. It could get tricky. Jack said that some people might not want to see history changed, and he was right. I'm not saying I want to change anything; I just have been given an extraordinary opportunity to reveal a cloaked piece of history. This is big! I have to know."

"You'll need me to show you all the stuff that came with the trunk. I don't remember it all, but I'll know it when I see it. Besides, I need to get back there and needle the old bitch across the street. It's been too long. HA!"

Wood slapped his leg as the anticipation showed in his face. "I found the family tree book this morning, by the way. It's in my suitcase. You can't see it if you don't let us go, so there."

Maggie looked at the little man she loved so dearly and shook her head. "Yeah, Grace misses you too, I'm sure." She gave her dad a big hug, then Wood reached down and grabbed a pillow.

"Hey Lovey!" Wood said, as he threw the pillow at the cross-legged woman on the floor. "Get your meditative ass up and let's get ready to fly."

"Maggie and I have business first," Lovey stated, coming out of a deep meditation.

Lovey rolled over, got up off the carpet, stood and reached out for Maggie's hand. "We gotta talk a bit. Trust me." With that, she proceeded to lead Maggie to a back bedroom. Maggie looked back over her shoulder at Jack and Wood, who just stood there in wonder as they disappeared into the room and closed the door.

"What's goin' on?" Jack asked, still staring at the door.

"Woman shit. I don't want to know. It is weird, though. That's where Lovey goes to do her meditations with clients. Something's up. Only one thing left to do. Bong time!"

Wood went straight to the couch where his bong and little baggie of pot were left from the night before.

"I can't get on an airplane straight. Not going to happen. Want a hit?"

Jack watched in amazement as Wood loaded his bowl and put the lighter to it. He glanced at the clock on the wall that read 9:15 am. "Man, this is a bad idea. Load me one."

Soon, Jack and Wood were as stoned as two teenagers skipping school. "Oh, shit! Jeanie's on!" Wood yelled, as he reached for the remote control. He ran through the channels and then landed on "I Dream of Jeanie" and said, "Hell yeah! A good breakfast, a good buzz and Jeanie. This is living."

Back in the bedroom was an entirely different scene. Lovey was sitting across from Maggie, both on old beanbag chairs, where Lovey had Maggie's outstretched arms in hers. Maggie wore a large black blindfold that cut her off from any reality in the room other than Lovey's voice. A small fan drowned out any noise from the outside.

"Just relax, darlin'. Close your mind off from everything around you. Let it all go. Listen to the dark." Lovey had Maggie relaxing and told her to feel her inner self as she guided her into a hypnotic state. Lovey began to speak in a low whisper. "I want you go back to the time of Daniel Blanch. Start with the sounds you are hearing. Look outside your window into the street. You remember it all like it was yesterday because it was yesterday when you were there.

You are in love with Elizabeth Kortright and you are going to see her today. She's so pretty and nice to you. You are in love with Elizabeth Kortright and you'll see her…today. You'll see her in an hour, you'll see her in a minute, you see her….. now."

Maggie seemed to hang there in suspension and then "Oh! Oh!!" She shuddered and clawed at the blindfold on her face ripping it off and looked around the room wide-eyed.

"Easy darlin'," Lovey said, as she grabbed Maggie's arm. "Easy now. You're just fine."

Maggie looked into the eyes of Lovey as her present reality took hold. "My God, I saw her! I swear I did. I saw Elizabeth. I saw Elizabeth Kortright. It was like I was there. I was with her. I'm telling you I could see her!"

"Calm down now," Lovey said softly. "Now tell me, what did you see?"

Maggie sat in a daze as she told of her experience. "It was like a dream, you know? I could hear and smell everything. The smells. Yeah, the smells were really strong. I could see myself walking down a path somewhere. When I got near some buildings, I went to a door and opened it. A bell rang. A small bell that told people someone had come in. Then there she was behind the counter. She looked right at me. I'm telling you she was real! She looked right at me! Holy shit. Did that happen? Did I really go there?"

"If you saw her, then you did. I had a feeling when I felt that ledger that it was connected to you somehow. I think it was yours, Mags. I have a strong sense that you are the reincarnation of Daniel Blanch. When you saw Elizabeth, you were reliving your experience from a past life. I'm saying your experience was a memory from your time as him."

Maggie stood up and shook herself off. "I don't believe it."

"Maggie, we are able to see many things from our past if we use a focal point. I gave you a specific scenario from Blanch's past life. I confess. Last night after you went to bed, I couldn't sleep thinking about that ledger. I went out to your car and read the last pages. I saw the power of that ledger and it was clear you had a connection. I suspected you were him. That's why I had to do this exercise. It was to see for sure what your connection is. Now we know that you are playing with fire."

Maggie seemed shaken by the revelation just handed her. "If I was him, then why is all this dangerous? I don't understand. If I've already been through all this, then why can't I relive it and find out more about the murder?"

"Don't you see? Look where you are. The book wants you here. The book reached out to you. It's no coincidence you found it. I'm telling you; something is very wrong about all this. You need to let this go."

"You know I can't do that now. I can't, not after seeing her. Not after being in front of her. I think I can do more. You have to hypnotize me again. You have to! I need to see her again!"

"Listen to yourself! You've seen her one time and already you're sounding obsessive. Blanch was that way toward her. Look what happened. He killed a man over her. This is fire, Maggie. I've seen this before. This is fire and fire burns. You need to drop this now."

Maggie felt lost. She had just been given a glimpse into another part of herself she had never known. The idea that she had just walked as Blanch in her mind was crazy, yet compelling. How could she not go back for more? She had to know more about Daniel Blanch and why she was called to find the ledger.

The two opened the door to the bedroom and stepped out into the aroma from freshly burned marijuana and sounds of laughter coming from the living room. Maggie and Lovey walked into find both Jack and Wood stoned as shit, watching Gilligan's Island.

Wood jumped up and said, "Lovey! It's the episode where they do the play! Do her! Come on. Show Jack. Do her, here she is!"

Lovey and Maggie got in front of the TV and could see Jim Backus and Natalie Schafer

(Thurston Howell III and Lovey from the cast) walking from their hut. Thurston said, "Lovey, where's Gilligan? He was supposed to me make a tennis racket." Lovey then put her hand on her hip and said, "Thuuuurston, dahling. I'd so adore a new racket. Have him make two."

Wood cut off the sound of the TV and looked at his girlfriend standing there with an annoyed look on her face. She cocked her hip and performed a perfect impression. Jack and Wood burst out laughing. "That's amazing!" Jack yelled. "It's just like her!" Maggie, you hear that? She could be her!"

Maggie gave a harsh look to the two and the situation. "I'm going to take a shower." And she left for the bedroom.

Wood and Jack watched her walk away. "What's got into her?" Jack asked.

Wood scratched his head and said, "I told you, we don't want to know."

As Maggie disappeared into the bathroom to take her shower, Wood said to Jack, "Come outside. I want you to meet the girls."

Jack followed Wood like a puppy. They went outside to his back yard where a variety of cages stood. The coo of pigeons could be heard as they approached.

"These are my girls." Wood said proudly. "They all come from great stock and can fly for days without a break. More dependable than the mailman."

Jack was fascinated. "So you don't use telephones at all?"

"Nope. Damned government is listening to everything we say."

"You sound a little paranoid there, Wood."

"It's the truth!" Wood said. "I know people who are doing time right now because of taps. I won't go there. My girls here go where they need to go and nobody knows what I send but me and the person at the other end of the run."

"Amazing," Jack said as he studied the birds. "It's old school."

"Lovey has her own birds over there," Wood said as he pointed to another set of cages. "They are a different breed than mine. Racers. We keep them separate. It gives us something to do. I know a kid up the street who feeds them for me while I'm gone. I'll let him know we are leaving. He has a few birds I got him started with. Watch."

Wood wrote a note on a small piece of paper and then took out one of his birds. He attached the note to the leg of the bird and threw it up in the air. It circled the house and flew around the neighborhood until descending on a house in the distance. "Just like that," Wood said proudly. "My neighbor will get the note, then feed the girls while we're away."

"How do they know where to go?" Jack asked.

"That's a secret only us bird guys know." Wood laughed.

Chapter 9

IT'S FRIED!

The view from the jet was awe-inspiring as the plane approached the Denver airport. Wood was wide-eyed looking down on the land. Maggie was still struggling with feelings awakened earlier in the day through her past life regression. Lovey was sitting with eyes closed, meditating for a safe landing. Jack was asleep. The morning 'television session' with Wood had taken its toll.

After a textbook landing, a bout with baggage claim, and renting a car, they were headed back to the Barn. The familiar surroundings brought Maggie out of her quiet reflection and she began to comment on the scenery. All seemed well. Even Jack had come back to earth.

"I missed this place," Wood said. "I figured I'd seen enough of it to last a lifetime. But man, it's been a while. Even the mountains look different."

"It's home, Dad. Always will be. Home always looks good," Maggie sighed. She let her mind go back to her vision earlier when she saw Elizabeth. Was that a distant home? Was that some place she needed to go back to? For someone who was so sure of herself, she was in a place of uncertainty. It would take time to unravel the answers.

As they made the final turn on their way back to the Barn, instead of the familiar parking lot they were met with two fire trucks and the Sheriff's car. Maggie Styles' Antique Barn had burned to the ground.

Wood yelled, "It's fried!"

Maggie took a deep breath and forgot to exhale.

Jack parked the car, and as they got out they heard, "Maggie!" come from across the street. Maggie was speechless. She scanned the carnage for anything salvageable and it appeared there was nothing. She turned to see Grace and Pete coming across the road.

"It went up like a bonfire," Grace said, as she hugged Maggie. "About three o'clock this morning our smoke alarms went off. We got up to see the light coming from your place and called down the mountain to the fire department. By the time they got here it was too late. All they could do was shoot what water they had in the trucks on what wasn't on fire yet. I'm so sorry, Maggie. We called your cell phone. Where were you?"

Grace heard a familiar voice. "What, you couldn't come blow it out yourself?" She turned to see Wood standing behind her. At that moment any aggressive banter Grace could muster went up with the still smoldering building in front of them. Grace reached out and hugged Wood with an embrace only they understood. "Come here you little shit. I'm so sorry, Wood. I know you spent years collecting all this."

"Sorry Maggie," was heard as Deputy Sam Hecker came up to her.

"Hello, Sam," Maggie said while still looking through the debris.

"Maggie, this doesn't make much sense. It went up like a rocket. We don't get too many arson cases up here, but it looks to me like somebody set this off. You make anybody mad lately?"

"No. Not that I know of. My customers are all over the place. UPS ships stuff outta here. Nobody I know would do this," Maggie said still standing in disbelief at the sight of her beloved business now gone.

Sam looked down at the ground and kicked a rock across the gravel and said, "Maggie, I got to ask you this. Where were you last night? Did you have anything to do with this? I guess you are insured. I've got to file a report and the insurance company is going to sure ask questions. I just want this all done formal so you don't get a run around from them, you understand?"

Jack walked over to Maggie and put his arm around her and said, "She was with me."

Maggie fell into Jack and started to cry. Wood and Lovey walked over to them and Wood said. "She was with us in Florida. She didn't have anything to do with this. How you been Sam?"

"Hey, Wood. Good to see you. Audrey, you too."

As Maggie and Jack walked back to the car, Jack whispered to her, "Is that Lovey's real name? Audrey?"

"Yeah, that's her name. Audrey Hecker. Sam and Pete are her brothers."

Jack stopped short. "What?" He turned around to look at the three standing there in a sort of family reunion. Nobody seemed glad to see anyone. It was weird.

"They don't look like family," Jack said.

"They have a long story. That's one of the reasons Lovey wanted to leave here. She and Wood took off and never looked back. It's old shit. Family crap that runs way deep."

Sam walked over to Maggie and looked at the still smoldering rubble. "You went to Florida? What for? You just decide to run off to see Wood and Audrey?"

Maggie was leaning on Jack when she said, "You met Jack the other night. He was heading back to Georgia and I paid him to take me the rest of the way to see Dad. It seemed like a good time. It's a long drive alone. My Jeep would have beat me to death by the time I got there."

"Oh, I get it," Sam said. "You know the Sheriff is going to want to talk to you about this, Maggie. There's going to be an investigation, you can bet."

"You say it looks like somebody started the fire? Where? What makes you think that?" Jack said.

"Come here and I'll show you." As Jack, Maggie and Sam walked to the back of the now charred and smoking Barn, Jack called out to Wood who was still talking to Pete and Grace. Wood then followed them all to see where Sam was taking them.

"See here?" Sam pointed to two melted plastic gasoline cans that were behind the rubble. "I guess who ever did this thought these plastic gas containers would burn up. It looks like the fire started from inside, but I can't figure how anybody could get in there without setting off the alarm. If somebody broke a window and poured all the gas that those two containers could hold in there, then all it would take was a spark from anywhere. That's the kind of thing the forensic boys will go through tomorrow, I guess. You could see the glow of the fire from all the way down the mountain."

Jack asked, "Who'd do this?" He looked at Maggie and said, "Hey, look at me. Tell me. Do you remember anyone being mad at you or saying anything that would make you think they wanted this place in flames to get back at you for something?"

"No!" Maggie said, now getting angry. "Nobody. Nobody at all."

"Could have been kids," Jack said coldly. "Little bastards do all kinds of stuff back home out of boredom."

"No kids here would do this," Sam confirmed. "No kids like that around here."

"Well, it sure as hell was somebody!" Jack barked.

"You need to stay around here for a while, Maggie. You're going to have to talk to some people about this," Sam warned as he walked away to the front, leaving Maggie, Jack and Wood there to assess the damage.

Lovey walked around to where they were and gave her condolences. "It's just not right. These were just old things. Why would anyone want to see them destroyed like this? All this way to get an old trunk and it's gone. It was a family heirloom as well. It's a shame."

Suddenly, Maggie remembered why they had come. The trunk. Maggie looked at Wood and Jack as they all three turned around to see the out building that was still standing, singed, but not burned. They all three at once walked over to it.

"The firemen must have soaked it so it wouldn't burn," Wood said. "Well, I'll be."

Maggie opened the door and they walked in. "It's back here," Maggie said to Wood as they walked into the musty building. As they reached the trunk Wood said, "There you are. That's it! Still ugly as it ever was."

"What else came with it Dad? Can you remember? Look around."

Lovey asked, "How can you remember what is in here?" as she tried to distance herself from all the dust.

Wood looked around at all the junk lying around them and said, "I don't see anything other than this old trunk."

Maggie seemed agitated. "Think Dad! Where would you have put things? It has to be in here because if anything was out in the barn, we're sunk."

A voice came from the doorway that startled them all.

"Maggie? You in here?" It was Sheriff Mack Rogers. "I can't see a thing."

Maggie yelled back, "Mack? We're back here!"

Jack, Maggie, Wood and Lovey all walked out to meet Mack. "How you doing Maggie? Sorry about the fire. Ho' Wood. Been a while. Audrey. Good to see you."

"Hello, Mack," Wood said as he shook hands with the Sheriff. "How's down the mountain?"

"Flat," Mack scoffed. Mountain people have a way of regarding time spent in the flatlands as not as worthy as time spent in the scenic mountains.

"Mack, you're handsome as ever. Come here you big hunk." Lovey gave Mack a very familiar hug. As she pulled away their eyes met and Jack got the feeling they had done that before.

"I'm Jack Reynolds," Jack said as he extended his hand. "I'm a friend of Maggie's."

"I already talked to Sam. He said there would be an investigation," Maggie said, turning on her 'damsel in distress' charm. "What can I do?"

"Just hang around town until the insurance folks show up. They are going to want to see all this. You can bet. If you're planning on going anywhere in the next few days, you better not. Lots of questions in an arson case. You up for this? It might get hairy."

Wood spoke up and said, "You know she didn't do this. She was with us in Florida. We drove in a while ago from the Denver airport and saw all the trucks and shit. I don't know who did it, but it wasn't Maggie."

"Maggie's a history professor," Mack said, looking at her as she surveyed the burned mess in front of them. "History professors don't burn up history, even if it is just old antiques in a building. You have my support on this. I'll vouch for your character, Mags. Just don't leave. Stay around here, back at your place. It'll look better if you cooperate and get this behind you. You thinking of re-building?"

Maggie stepped back and looked all around. "I...I haven't even swallowed this yet. I have no idea what I'll do. We just got here a few minutes ago. I haven't had to time think about it."

"Good answer!" Mack said. "Usually people that burn their own businesses are doing it so they can re-model from the insurance money. That clearly isn't your intention. It's all good Maggie. You should be OK after all this. I'm sorry. I'll be at the Grizzly if you need me. You folks hungry? Grace has pot roast today."

"I'll just stay here for a bit," Maggie said. "There's nothing left here. You have my information. Call me if you need me."

"I'm going over to the Grizz. Been awhile. Lovey, you comin'?" Wood escorted Lovey across the gravel parking lot. Jack and Maggie just stood there looking at the smoldering ashes in disbelief.

Chapter 10

THE FAMILY TREE

It was getting late when the four left the charred remains of Maggie Styles' Antique Barn. "Where to?" Jack asked as he left the parking lot.

"I just want to go home," Maggie sighed, as she got one last glimpse of who she used to be, now lost in the charred remains.

As they pulled up to Maggie's house on the side of the mountain, the view was awesome. You could see for miles into the valley below. "The place needs paint," Wood observed as he got out. "Seems like I just had it done."

"You have her house painted, Wood? What a dad!" Jack exclaimed as he looked up at the two-story Victorian house. It looked like a picture from a post card.

Maggie told Jack, "This was Dad's house before it was mine. It came with the Barn."

"At least you still got the house," Wood reminded her.

Maggie walked in the front door and went straight out onto her back deck. She stood there looking over the valley that fell before her and remembered the day she decided to buy the Barn from her dad. It was a big step; one she'd never regretted. Not even now, as the memory of the burned-out remains haunted her, did she regret buying it. The experience had introduced her to countless people across the country and made her a respected source in Antiques. She couldn't help but notice the last things the

Barn gave her were a pamphlet written by James Monroe, which she was sure she could sell, a two-hundred-year-old mystery, and Jack.

Jack walked out behind her and the two stood silently as the afternoon breeze blew the mountain trees into a kind of "shhhhhh." It seemed as though even the trees were trying to comfort her.

Jack looked at the side of her face to see a tear roll down.

"I can't tell you how sorry I am for all this, Maggie. I know you loved your place. I just can't believe someone would do this."

Looking out over the valley, Maggie sighed and said, "I've got to make some phone calls, I guess. Better get the insurance nightmare started."

Jack tried to comfort her. "Take a minute, for cryin' out loud. You just got some bad news. It's OK to be human."

"What do you want me to do, Jack? Stand here and sob because my livelihood just got smoked? I can't do that. It's not in me to be that broken person. I appreciate your sympathy, but it's not me. I gotta do this my way."

Maggie walked back inside leaving Jack out on the deck not knowing what to do next. Wood and Lovey came out and looked around at the trees.

Wood admitted, "I missed this place. Don't tell her. I was here thirty years and it seems like a minute ago." Wood looked in the house at Maggie now on the phone to the insurance company. "She'll be OK. Big trooper, that one. I hate to see that old place go. I wonder who lit that match. Had to be someone from up here, but I can't think of a soul who didn't like Mags."

Lovey reasoned, "Whoever did it is probably long gone. I loved that old place, too, but I think it was just a traveling fire bug who saw the old Barn as a target. You hear about these things all the time, you know? Some fool travels around looking for places to burn. They catch them eventually, as long as they keep burning, that is."

Jack told Lovey and Wood he felt bad for Maggie.

"It's weird that I show up, we find the ledger and all, then this. It's too strange."

Looking off into the valley Wood agreed.

"I hear ya! Something ain't right. I got a feelin' shit's about to get deep. Jack, come downstairs with me a minute, I'll show you the house."

Jack and Wood ventured through the hallways. Wood shared stories of each room and why it was a special place. Jack couldn't help but remember his own home and how he lived with his parents until he left for college. He hadn't been around any family atmosphere for some time. As the two walked down the stairs into the basement, Wood was looking around inspecting every detail. He then walked over to an old bookshelf where more antiques were stored, reached onto the shelf and got an old ceramic teakettle.

Jack asked, "What is that for? Is it teatime in Colorado?"

"No, but its buzz time!"

Wood reached in his pocket and pulled out an ounce of pot. "Where'd you get that? You didn't take that on the plane did you?" Jack asked, as a slight sense of alarm came over him seeing the baggie half filled with marijuana buds.

"Hell no!" Wood said. "Good ol' Pete. He grows some great shit!"

"His brother is a deputy and Pete grows weed? Why does that not surprise me? Man, Maggie's in a bad place. I can't get high now. Neither can you."

As Jack finished his sentence, Wood had loaded the ceramic bowl and had a lighter igniting the awaiting bud. As he inhaled, a crackling sound came from the burning weed. "Too late!" Wood said as he inhaled the pot and offered it to Jack. "Hit it quick before it goes out," Wood instructed still holding in his first hit.

"Shit man, this is just wrong." Jack reached out and took the bowl from Wood and hit it hard to keep it lit. "Shit!" Jack said, trying not to cough as the smoke came faster than expected.

The two stayed down in the basement for half an hour going through old antiques and giggling like kids.

"We'd better go up," Jack finally said. "I'm hammered! You say Pete grew this?"

Jack was holding both rails on the staircase. He inched his way up into the land of the living, where Maggie and Lovey seemed in a deep conversation.

"We're back!" Wood announced. "You get everything squared with the insurance company?"

"It's all phoned in," Maggie said. "They'll be in touch in the next couple of days. Where've you been?"

"Looking at some of the stuff in the basement," Wood said. "I still got some good pieces down there."

"Yeah, you do. You see any old tools down there, Jack? I don't go down there. No reason to except to change a fuse now and then. Speaking of old tools Dad, where is that family tree book you said you had? I wanted to look through it," Maggie asked, as she shot Lovey a quick glance.

"I'll get it." Wood went into the bedroom to get the book leaving the stoned-as-hell Jack standing in the line of Maggie and Lovey's stare.

Lovey looked at Jack and noticed his state.

"You OK Jack? You look a little peaked….wait a minute, have you been downstairs with Wood? You smoked some pot, didn't you?"

Jack just stood there. "Busted! I gotta get some water," he said as he turned to walk into the kitchen. Lovey and Maggie just looked at each other shaking their heads.

Jack wandered into the kitchen and came across a box of chocolate chip cookies. Jack tore open the box as Lovey and Maggie watched him eat three cookies in a row before looking up.

"These fuckers are killer! I haven't had these in years."

Lovey scoffed, "He's a real catch there, Maggie."

Maggie was at least sympathetic.

"It's Dad's fault! You know it. He's a bad influence on him. He's just trying to get along,"

Wood returned with the book of their family tree. The three sat down and began to turn the pages of the timetable that was Maggie's lineage.

"Glad I brought this," Wood said, as the pages slowly went by.

There were old pictures of relatives dating back to the 1800's. "We gotta find Blanch," Maggie said as she turned pages back to the time period. There was a tintype of a man and a woman with a small child in the last entry.

Maggie read aloud, "Bartholomew Campbell (Father: Gabriel Campbell, Mother: Rose Marie Jenkins), Pamela Blanch Campbell (Father: Daniel Theodore Blanch, Mother: Hope Carter Blanch), child: Mary Campbell."

"Here they are! Blanch, his wife and his daughter, Pamela. It's true! I am related to him. Jack, come and see this. I'm related the man who killed James Monroe!"

"See?" Wood said. "It's the Blanch branch. I told you."

Jack came over and sat down next to Maggie. He looked down at the book and tintype and said, "She's ugly as a barrel full of ass holes!" Then he busted out laughing. Wood fell back onto couch and put a pillow over his face and tried to hide his own laughter.

"Damn it! This is important and you guys are stoned as shit!" Maggie barked.

"Not my fault!" Jack said now catching his breath. "It was him! He did it!" Now pointing at Wood.

"Guilty," Wood muffled from beneath the pillow as he held up one finger.

Maggie studied the writing as much as she could. There it was. What could all this mean? Lovey was staring at her from across the room now. They both shared an "I told you so!" moment. Maggie looked at Wood and said, "You got any more of that, Dad? I just found out my great, great, whatever grandfather killed the man I did my thesis on and my business burned down last night. I could use a hit myself about now."

Chapter 11

THE INSURANCE
INSPECTORS ARRIVE

The next morning, Maggie and Jack awoke to the sound of the doorbell. It was 8:10 AM and the morning had come too soon.

Jack groaned, "Who the hell is that?"

"I haven't a clue," Maggie replied as she got up and put on her robe. "I'm fixing to find out."

Jack watched Maggie leave the room and rolled over to put his face in a pillow. "Great! Visiting hours have begun."

Maggie went to the door and could see a man and a woman through the window. She opened the door and the woman said, "Maggie Styles?"

"Yes, I'm Maggie," came her morning reply.

"We are from the Pate Insurance Company. We're here about your claim. I'm Sue Holden and this is Mark Williams. I know it's early, but we need to have a word with you about the fire."

Maggie abruptly remembered her situation.

"Oh, come on in." Maggie stepped back for the two to pass. Mark came in first and as Sue was about to enter, Maggie reached down to take the doorknob in her hand to close the door and her robe came falling open, revealing her nakedness underneath. Sue's eye immediately went down Maggie's front. As Maggie instinctively closed her robe Sue looked up at her and their eyes met. It was not a casual glance. There was something more in Sue's eyes than a simple "ooops." It was a stare of not more than three seconds, but it was enough. It was clear to them both that another agenda was at hand.

"I'm sorry, I just woke up," Maggie began. "I'll make some coffee. Did you go by the Barn?"

"Barn?" Mark said.

"Oh, that's what we call it. What's left of it. 'Maggie Styles' Antique Barn.' I still can't believe it's gone."

Mark began the inspector banter like a scene from an old Dragnet television show.

"Do you have any idea who did this, Miss Styles? Do you have any enemies or has anyone threatened you lately?"

Maggie was casually making coffee.

"No, and call me Maggie. I can't think of a soul who would do this. Do you think it was arson?"

The two inspectors sat at the table while Maggie moved about the kitchen in front of a large window. The sunlight was coming through and the thin white robe Maggie had on was revealing her figure beneath it. It was as if she was nude at times when she leaned over into the light. Neither Mark nor Sue bothered to mention it as they each were clearly entranced at her natural beauty.

"We went by there earlier. There was evidence of arson, Maggie," Sue said as she studied Maggie's reaction. "The melted gasoline canisters behind the building are clearly suspicious. The police report says you were in Florida with your father, his girlfriend, and a Jack Reynolds?"

"Yes. Jack and I went down to see Dad and Lovey, I'm mean Audrey. Lovey's a nickname. When we came back, we found the place burned."

Sue continued. "How long were you there?"

"Just overnight, really," Maggie answered, as she began to feel more in control.

"So, you drove down?"

"Yes, Jack and I took a couple of days to drive to Florida and then we flew back."

Mark began to stir as if he'd found something.

"So, who is Jack Reynolds?"

"He's a friend, I guess, maybe more. We've just met."

"Just met when?" Mark asked.

"A few days ago. Why?"

"So, you meet a man and all of a sudden you want to drive for what, two days to see your father, then stay overnight and fly back? While you are gone, your business burns to the ground with two gas canisters found on the scene. I'm sorry Maggie, but this string of events isn't playing out exactly in your favor."

Maggie stopped her moving about the kitchen and turned to face the two inspectors.

"In my favor? Do you think I was involved? I loved that place! My dad and I spent years collecting that entire inventory. It was his whole life! Why on earth would I just up and burn it? It was lucrative. It made me enough money to live comfortably up here. I own this house; I own my Jeep and I'm not in debt. All my school loans are paid. I guess at my age I'm an oddity because I don't owe anyone anything. So why would I all of a sudden decide to destroy all that? I'm no detective but I'm not stupid either."

"No, you're not stupid at all." Mark takes his clipboard and begins to read. "Your bio is on your website. It says here you were a college professor. You have a masters in U.S History and you taught at Tennessee. Why'd you leave to come up here?"

Maggie was beginning to become agitated. She walked over to the window and said, "Think of a classroom. You're teaching kids who don't give a shit about History, you're closed up all day and grading papers half the night. Now, look out there. Look at that view. Where would you want to be?"

If Maggie had suddenly subpoenaed ten witnesses, they could not have been more convinced. She had them there. Why would someone so in love with her surroundings want to suddenly erase it all? It didn't make sense. Sue and Mark were good at what they did. They'd read many faces and broken a lot of cases, but it was clear to them that if Maggie had anything to do with this case, she did it unknowingly. Or, she was a good actress.

Sue seemed on her side. "I see your point," She got up to walk over to the window and looked out over the valley, and then she glanced at Maggie's model-like face. "I'd love to see more," she offered as the two women had a momentary stare down.

"I'd love to show it to you." Maggie then slowly walked to the back door and opened it. "It's nice out here in the mornings." Maggie motioned for the two to go outside and experience the mountain morning. "Go on out. I'll bring the coffee."

Sue and Mark walked out on the deck as Maggie poured three cups of coffee and put them on a tray. "I don't know," Mark said to Sue. "If she had anything to do with that fire, I can't tell it. She sure plays the damsel in distress to a tee. With a body like that it's hard to concentrate on anything. You think that's on purpose?"

"What's on purpose?" Sue asked turning to Mark.

"Her wearing that next to nothing robe. You think that's to throw us off?"

Sue jumped to Maggie's defense.

"She just got up, Mark. She grabbed a robe, came to the door and here we are. I really don't think she planned for us to sit and think about her body while we interviewed her. She's smart, yeah, but give her a break. I just don't see it."

Mark gave Sue a look and smiled. "You like her, don't you? I can see it. That, 'I'd love to see more.' Please! I know you. You're hornier than I am. Don't let your sex drive cloud you here, Holden. Yeah, she's hot as a stovetop, but we got a job to do. Now focus on something here besides her tits."

Maggie came out on the deck with the coffee. "Here you go. I'm a big coffee drinker. Can't get started without it."

"Maggie, we want this off our screen as fast as possible," Mark said as he took the coffee cup. "You say you don't know a soul who would do this? An old angry student, perhaps? You had to have broken a few hearts back in the classroom. Can you think of any old grudges at all?"

"None. I got along well with all my students. They were all typical college people."

The door opened and Wood and Lovey came out onto the deck. "Oh, shit! Company! I thought I heard the doorbell ring."

"Dad, this is Sue Holden and Mark Williams. They are from the insurance company about the fire. Mark, Sue, this is my dad and his girlfriend, Audrey."

"Hi ya'! Call me Wood. Everyone does."

As handshakes are done, Lovey and Wood sat down with the inspectors and went over the same questioning with Jack finally emerging from his pillow to join them. After an introduction, he too was drawn into the circle. It was frustrating for Sue and Mark. It appeared this would be a long investigation.

As Sue and Mark turned to leave, Mark told Maggie, "We'll be in touch. You aren't planning on going anywhere any time soon, I hope?"

"Why do you ask?" Maggie said as if her parents had just grounded her.

"Because this is an investigation, Maggie. We need to have access to you and all your files, documents, bank data, the works. We want to find out who did this. The forensic guys will be here this afternoon. After we see what they find, this will probably officially be listed as an arson case. That means a lot of work. Until we conclude that you had nothing to do with it, no payout will happen. You'll get no money from us until this is settled."

"But I thought we just established that I wasn't involved," Maggie said, now obviously annoyed.

"Look, we want to believe you," Sue started. "But,

regardless of what we think, everything has to be properly documented. We don't issue money, someone else in some other department does that."

Maggie seemed obviously hurt and scared by all this accusation. Sue turned and told Mark she'd meet him at the car. Mark seemed put off by this, and grudgingly went out and leaned on the door.

"Don't worry about all this coming at you at once," Sue began. "It's just procedure. We show up and go through the process. That's our job. We will let you know this afternoon about the official report. If you think of anything and want to talk, you can call me here." Sue handed Maggie her business card, and, as she did, Maggie's hand came off her robe. Once more it fell open, only this time Maggie didn't close it as fast. "I'm looking forward to seeing you again, Maggie," Sue said as their eyes once more locked.

"It'll be a pleasure, I'm sure," Maggie said as she slowly closed her robe.

As Sue walked back to the car, Maggie stood at the door and watched Sue's ass move under her wide hips. Sue knew she was watching her and made every step count as she slinked towards the car. As she reached it, she threw a glace and a smile over her shoulder to Maggie in the doorway. As Sue got in the car, she was met with Mark saying, "You are way out of line on this Holden. We don't fuck the suspects, even if they are out of this world hot. Did you see her? God, what a body!"

"Yeah. I saw her. I saw her real well. I plan on seeing a lot more of her when this is done. I haven't felt that attracted towards a woman in a long time. That is one hot lady." Sue thought out loud.

Mark was being blunt. "Then you admit it! You want to fuck her?"

"Hell yeah I admit it!" Sue confessed. "Anybody would! I saw you watching her through that robe. Don't tell me it didn't cross your mind and don't play choirboy with me, Williams. I know you too."

Maggie also felt something towards Sue. She liked her. It

was her directness, her confidence, her ass. She turned to see Jack behind her and blushed as though she'd been caught doing something naughty.

"You OK? You think it'll all be alright?" Jack's eyes had a sympathetic glow that Maggie needed. She fell into him and put her arms around his neck. Her emotions had been stirred by Sue and found her body tingling to the touch. She'd gotten up too early and had a sense of sleep deprivation hanging over her. That, coupled with her horny state, made her whisper in Jack's ear, "Let's go back to bed."

Jack leaned back and looked over his shoulder at Wood cooking one of his morning feasts and Lovey out on the deck, cross-legged in a soon-to-be state of meditation. "You sure? Now?"

"Yea, now," Maggie said as she took his hand and slipped it into her open robe, down to where Sue was focusing just moments before. Maggie inhaled deeply as he touched her, then she reached down, took his hand and led him back to their bedroom. They were going to be late for breakfast.

Chapter 12

SOMETHING
TO LOOK FORWARD TO

Later that afternoon the four were sitting out on the deck with the ledger from the trunk and the family tree book Wood had found. Jack had re-read the ledger and was puzzled by the phrase, "I hid it here and nobody gon no."

"Why would Blanch say where he was hiding the notebook he took off James Monroe when he killed him? It doesn't make sense. If he were hell bent on no one finding it, why would he say he was hiding it 'here'? He would have been opening up the possibility of someone finding out he had killed a man in cold blood. His whole existence at this point was dependent on people not finding that out and he said, 'I hid it here'. Now why would a man as smart as Blanch say that? It doesn't add up. It would have to have been a great hiding place. Now, where would that be in an old house in 1802?"

Lovey reminded him, "It also said that he was dying, Jack. If the man knew he was dying, maybe he wanted the notebook to be found. Maybe he wanted to clear his conscience that he'd committed a murder."

"No, not him." Jack continued. "Not Blanch. It says in your family tree that Blanch married a woman named Hope and had a daughter. Pamela was it? That gives him a legacy. His kid. He wouldn't risk anyone finding the notebook because it was too important to him. He wouldn't just give away the location."

Lovey looked over at Maggie who was sipping a wine cooler and staring off into space. "Mags, when did the inspectors say they would get in touch with you about the arson thing?"

"This afternoon," Maggie began. "That's all I know. I'm staying here. I see no point in going over there and stirring things up. If they want to charge me with arson then they can damned well do it. I didn't have a thing to do with that fire. Nothing."

"Speak of the devil and he appears," Wood said as he heard activity coming up the driveway. "Holy shit! It's everybody! The Sheriff, Pete, Grace and those two from this morning. This doesn't look good."

"It looks like it looks," Jack said. "If they are here to take Maggie, they'll have to take her through me."

"Stop it! Let's do this. I'm not hiding or running. I'm innocent," Maggie proclaimed. When they heard the doorbell ring, the four got up and went to the door together to find Mark and Sue followed by the rest.

"Maggie Styles," Sue began. "After an investigation of your property the forensic team hired by your insurance company has determined that the fire in Maggie Styles' Antique Barn was by all accounts…. a case of faulty wiring. Therefore, Pate Insurance Company will have no charges brought against you in this matter. You will receive full insurance benefits from our company after you sign some forms."

"What? No charges?" Maggie exclaimed with relief. She then turned to Jack, Lovey and Wood who were all standing speechless behind her and they all yelled out at once, "Yes!!"

Shortly afterwards, everyone was sitting out on the deck having a 'Yay Maggie!' party. "I thought I was in deep shit," Maggie told Sue.

"I thought you were as well; I have to say."

"What about the red gas containers behind the place? Didn't that point to some kind of foul play?"

Sue concluded, "I would have thought so, but Pete over there, who cuts your grass, testified to the police and the arson investigators that he left those containers there by mistake. When the fire started, it just set them off and they melted." Standing up, she told Maggie, "I've got to go to the ladies' room. Be right back."

As Sue walked across the room, Maggie turned to see Pete who she knew had never cut her grass. Not once. She always cut it herself. Pete caught her gaze and held up his beer in a triumphant manner, nodded his head, and went back to his conversation.

"I need a wine cooler," Maggie sighed as she got up to go inside. She went to the refrigerator, got out a wine cooler, opened it and then turned to see Sue standing outside the bathroom. She wasn't saying anything, just standing there. Then, ever so slightly, she licked her lips. Maggie glanced outside at the crowd on the deck and then slowly walked towards her. Sue didn't move. As Maggie reached her, she leaned forward and whispered in Sue's ear, "You want to see the basement?" Maggie turned to go down the steps leading into the dark room below. Sue never said a word but followed her down the steps. When they reached the end the smell of pot hit them hard.

"Dad's been down here," Maggie said with a chuckle.

Sue looked around the dimly lit room and said, "Smells like someone smoked a...." Maggie turned around. Buzzed from the wine coolers, she reached out and touched Sue's bottom lip, interrupting her from her thought. Maggie pulled the lip down ever so slightly and then Sue opened her mouth and began to suck on Maggie's finger. Maggie stepped into her pushing her thigh between Sue's legs, feeling the warm center. Sue cocked her head sideways, Maggie removed her finger and replaced it with her mouth. It was a deep kiss that they both had anticipated. Sue's arms went around Maggie's neck as she pulled her in. Maggie let her soft lips run up and down Sue's neck as she bent her head as far over as it would go.

"You got me wet this morning," Sue whispered. "That robe you had on was driving me insane. I could see through it against the window. You look so beautiful in the light."

Maggie kept kissing her neck up and down. She then reached down and took both of Sue's hands and placed them on her breasts. Sue's mouth went to Maggie's as she let her hands rub circles around Maggie's chest. Maggie then leaned back, pulled up her shirt and lifted her bra letting her large, perfect breasts fall free. Sue put her hands back as she bowed her head down to the soft skin. Maggie gasped, reached down between Sue's legs and began to massage her crotch through her pants.

Maggie unsnapped Sue's pants, unzipping them so they fell open. She slipped her hand easily into Sue's panties and felt the soft warmth. Sue was about to howl. Maggie started to rub her gently at first, then faster and faster. Sue was boiling. "Oh, God!" was all she could say. Then "Oh God, I'm...." She began to shudder as Maggie kept her hand moving in a perfect non-stop motion until Sue's hand gently stopped her to let the spasms from her climax subside.

Maggie whispered to her, "Shhhhh. Shhhhhh. Let it out. Shhhhhhhh."

Sue fell back against the wall and then gave Maggie a deep kiss. She had fallen in as deep as she had ever dared to go with another woman. Maggie was her dream girl. She was smart, beautiful and an uninhibited lover.

Maggie put her clothes back together then whispered in Sue's ear, "We've got to go back upstairs."

"But what about you? Let me take care of you," Sue begged.

Maggie smiled at Sue and kissed her again. "Later. Not now. It'll give me something to look forward to."

As Maggie began to walk up the stairs, Sue was left in a shaken dilemma. "It'll give me something to look forward to," kept ringing in her mind over and over. She watched Maggie's perfect frame ascend the staircase and told herself she would soon be with that body again. Next time, even more intimate. She suddenly wanted to come again at the thought of it. She had just had a monster orgasm, now, she had to go back up and face the world. One thing was for sure; this was one day she really liked her job.

When Maggie reached the top of the stairs she slipped into the bathroom. When she came out, she ran into Sheriff Rogers. Startled, she said, "Well hi, Mack. You surprised me."

"I surprised you just now, or when I pulled up with the inspectors and the news you'd been exonerated?" Mack said as he looked for Maggie's reaction.

"Well, I've got to admit I was worried," Maggie admitted. "We all were. The evidence at first glance was leaning the other way. I'm not sure how it went back in my favor but I'm deeply grateful to whatever force it was that did it."

Mack turned to see the others out on the deck. He was about to speak when he heard Sue coming up the stairs. "It's creepy down there!" Sue said, seeing Mack. "Maggie said there were other antiques down there, but I saw nothing I wanted other than an old tea kettle. That for sale, Maggie?"

"It's Dad's. Ask him," Maggie replied. "He's had it for years." As Sue walked away Maggie turned back to Mack and asked, "You got something else to say?"

"Maggie, you know and I know that a fire at your place was as likely as boobs on a boar! Something isn't right here. Pete told the inspectors he cut your grass. That's bullshit and you know it. Pete doesn't even cut his own grass. Grace cuts it. Is there something you know you're not telling us?"

"Mack, we pulled up yesterday and my livelihood was burned to shit. I was in Florida seeing Dad the day before. Now here we are. I'd like to talk to the forensic guys myself, but hey, I just got cleared of this and the last thing I want to do is jump back into the frying pan. I know you can understand that. Why Pete said he cut my grass, I can't tell you. Ask him. I intend to, but I got to say, I don't know whether to question him or thank him."

"I'll be looking around, Maggie. I don't like loose ends. This fire is one big one," Mack said, giving her the eye.

"Lovey, I mean Audrey, I'll never get used to calling her Audrey, said it was probably some roving fire bug who goes from town to town setting fires," Maggie remembered. "Why don't you look to see if any other fires have been set in the area lately? If they have the same M.O. then you have something. I know I didn't have shit to do with it. I was in the black. No debt. No reason to destroy anything. I've repeatedly said that. If you want to keep searching, go ahead. If you find something, I'm all ears. For now, I'm getting another wine cooler."

Maggie walked to the refrigerator then went outside. Mack watched her, then went into the bathroom. Jack was sitting by the rail looking out at the view, still buzzed from his trip to the basement with Wood.

"This is crazy great! I can't think of anywhere I've ever been that is more beautiful than this. Look at this," he said, as he held out his arm in a majestic gesture. "I give you, God's country." Just then his phone rang. He looked down and saw it was Seth, his boss. "Shit, I gotta take this. I'm hammered, too." Maggie smiled as she watched Jack take his phone and slip inside the house.

"Hello? This is Jack Reynolds. I'm on vacation, remember?" Jack said as he answered the phone.

"Jack! You with Maggie Styles?" It was Paris, Jack's co-worker at Holiday Cabins in Georgia.

"Well, yeah, sort of. She's on the deck, why?"

"Jack? Hey buddy." Jack could hear Seth in the background. "We're on speaker."

"Ok. What's up?" Jack asked, as he imagined the two by the phone.

"We did some checking on your new girlfriend, Maggie Styles."

"You did what? Why in hell did you do that?" Jack asked as the conversation began a left-hand turn.

Seth admitted, "I had a feeling something was weird about her, Jack. I had Paris run a check and guess what? There turned out to be a lot more to her than we thought."

Paris jumped in and said, "Seth asked me to do it, Jack. It wasn't my idea."

"OK, regardless of whose idea it was, why are you two calling me?"

Paris began with, "When I Googled 'Maggie Styles' a

few things came up pertaining to her antique place. No big deal. Then, when I went to run the same background check we run on applicants on her and guess what came up?"

"I'm all ears," Jack said waiting for the shoe to fall.

"Nothing," Paris said. "I got nada, Jack. I checked public records to find out whose name was on the lease for Maggie Styles' Antique Barn. It didn't show Maggie Styles buying the place from a Lester P. Long. It's Abigail Long who bought it first, Lester's daughter, then Maggie Styles. I did some digging and found out Abigail Long was a history professor at The University of Tennessee."

"Yeah," Jack said. "Maggie told me she had a masters in American History and taught there."

"That's right. There was an Abigail Long listed as a Professor there for five years. Not Maggie Styles. I went to the Tennessee state records and there is an Abigail Long with a picture of your girlfriend above it. Abigail Long had her name changed to Maggie Styles after she got charged."

"Charged with what?" Jack said now fully attentive.

"Murder, Jack," Seth contributed from the back of the room. "Your new angel face girlfriend has a murder charge on file against her."

"What?" Jack barked.

Just then, the sheriff came out of the bathroom and walked towards Jack. He stopped talking and went into a smiling mode as the sheriff walked by. "Trouble at the office," Jack whispered as he rolled his eyes. After the sheriff walked through the glass door, "What murder charge? You have the wrong person, Paris. There is no way the girl I'm with is a murderer."

"It was circumstantial, Jack. She was with a student having some hot teacher/student fling and then the kid disappeared. He just vanished and nobody has seen him since."

"That doesn't mean Maggie's a murderer just because some college kid goes missing. For crying out loud, Paris!"

"That's not the end of it, Jack. It's not just one kid. It's four! Four kids, three guys and a girl were all rumored to have been having hot sex with Abigail Long and then, one by one, they all just left the face of the earth. No idea where any of them went. Charges were filed against her and it was all ruled circumstantial. No victim, no crime."

Jack looked through the sliding glass door at the woman he had fallen so in love with these past few days. "No way. I don't buy it. She's a sweetheart! Smart, funny. I'd know if she was a killer, for God's sake."

"Would you know if she was ever in a mental institution, Jack?" Paris asked coldly.

Jack held the phone for a moment until what Paris had just said hit home. "A mental institution? She told me she left teaching to come up here and buy the antique business from her dad."

"She did," Paris continued. "She left teaching, left Tennessee and went to a mental rehabilitation facility in Fredericksburg, Virginia."

Jack felt a cold shiver run down his spine. Fredericksburg was the place where Blanch had written the ledger.

"Holy God!" Jack said. "Did you say Fredericksburg?"

"Yeah, Bowden Psychiatric. It's a departmental facility at Mary Washington Hospital in Fredericksburg, Virginia. Why?"

Jack stood quiet again. "Jack? You there?"

Jack took a deep breath as though he was about to tell someone to hit him for fun.

"Never mind. How long was she there?"

"I found some records in an old public file that said she was there fourteen months, then moved to Colorado to buy the antique barn. She bought it as Abigail Long until the paperwork went through for her name change. Then it was all re-done to Maggie Styles. I tried to hack the nut house data bank but I hit a big firewall. I have a friend who can hack it if we pay him. He's smart as shit, but greedy."

Seth chimed in from the back of the room. "How greedy? What'll it cost to get the records?"

"Probably a few hundred bucks. He's good, though. He's been trying to date me for months. He can do a clean hack, in and out, no problem."

"Do it," Seth said. "Get Romeo to get the files."

Jack was listening on the other end and said, "Seth, man, she's not crazy. I've been with this woman and we have a connection. I'm telling you, she's not a crazed killer. I appreciate the dough but save it. Let me see what's up here in a few days. We are on a sort of treasure hunt."

"Treasure hunt?" Paris asked. "What kind of treasure hunt?"

"Oh, it's nothing. We found an old book and we're following some things written in it for a laugh. Nothing big."

Paris was curious. "Jack, does she take any medication? Like, in the mornings, does she take any pills? Have you seen any prescription bottles? If she was in an institution, chances are she's on meds to keep her sane. Watch her and see if she's on anything."

Jack was trying to remember if he'd seen Maggie taking any medication over the last two days and couldn't remember anything. He was suddenly sweating.

Paris confirmed, "I'll call my friend and we'll set up the hack, We need those records. I'd tell you just to walk away from her, but it sounds like you won't."

"Forget about her, Jack. Sounds like she could be dangerous. Be careful out there. I'll have Paris call you if we find out anything more."

Jack heard himself say, "Okay, bye," but his head was somewhere else. His mind was swirling. He looked out at Maggie, or Abigail, or whoever she was, and all doubt went away. He'd fallen in love with her and there was no going back. He had to ride this out as long it took. He had to know if this woman was indeed the woman of his dreams or his worst nightmare.

Chapter 13

PARIS AND THE SNOWMAN

Paris arrived at 776 Baxter Street at 7:30pm with a weird feeling about going to a guy's house that she had continually said "no" to. Paris only knew this guy online as a fellow hacker, and a good one. He had a reputation for getting in and out of targeted computer systems clean, without ever being tracked. His handle was "The Snowman" supposedly because he could just melt away without a trace. He knew her only as "Cody", as most hackers shadow themselves in a degree of anonymity online. She assumed he knew a lot more about her than she knew about him. After all, he was The Snowman. Walking up to his front door, she was worried that even snowmen leave a carrot and some coal once in a while. Paris hoped this wouldn't be the case.

The bell rang, and her guy came to the door looking more like a "before" picture in a shaving cream ad than a computer nerd. After a casual greeting they went inside. Paris couldn't help but snicker at his lame attempt at a cool guy persona. There was a Miami Vice poster on the wall from the eighties that showed the star, Don Johnson, standing by his Ferrari. Paris giggled as she passed it. The Snowman had his shirt halfway unbuttoned like the character on the poster. Paris still wasn't going out with him.

"So, what are we into tonight, Cody? I got to get the dough up front. You know the drill. That is unless you'll have dinner with me on Saturday night. I give discounts to hot hackers, you know."

"I can't go out with you. I don't even know your real name. I have a rule; I never go out with anonymous people."

"If I tell you my real name will you go out with me? You'd be in an elite group of people who actually know who The Snowman is. How can you pass that up?"

Paris reached into her pocket and felt Seth's money and then an idea hit her. She could keep the money and go out with this super hacker, maybe she'd even pick up a few tricks along the way, get a free dinner out of it and impress her boss all at the same time. She then looked at the unshaved man next to her with his out of place halfway-unbuttoned shirt and said, "Here's five hundred."

After taking the money, he turned to his computer screen and said, "Fuck it. Call me 'Steven.' So, where to tonight little Cody? Or can I just call you 'Paris?'"

"Call me what you want to. I figured you knew my real name, by the way," Paris said, trying not to act impressed. "Your real name is Steven. Funny, I would have never guessed that. It seems too normal for you. Here's the hack."

Paris handed him the name and address of the Bowden Psychiatric Center in Fredericksburg, Virginia. "It's a departmental facility at Mary Washington Hospital," Paris added.

Realizing his digital destination, Steven admitted, "Hospitals are not easy hacks. They want to keep shit quiet in most of them. Lots of insurance hocus-pocus goes on in hospitals. I would assume psych wards are no different, maybe worse. Never hacked one before."

"Can you do it?" Paris asked now showing her anxiousness.

"Of course I can do it. That's not the issue. It's what I need to look for when I get there that I need to know."

"Medical records for Abigail Long," Paris answered. "I need to know what she was in there for, how long, was she cured of what ever it was that put her there, anything you can find."

Steven was now curious. "What's so important about Abigail that you want me to hack her records? She a good guy or a bad guy?"

With a noticeable degree of uncertainty in her voice, Paris said, "Let's just say that she's a mysterious guy. Or girl. You call it what you want."

"Well okay, let the game begin!" Steven announced as he went to work.

Fifteen minutes later Paris was holding a printout of Abigail Long's medical and psychiatric records from Virginia. Paris's jaw dropped at what she read. "This is perfect. I knew she was too good to be true!"

"Who is this for?" Steven asked as he watched her eyes grow wide with each page she read.

"Let's just say a friend of mine is about to find out a lot about his new girlfriend," Paris said as she collected her things. "Thanks. You really helped me out here. This is big!"

As Paris went to the door she turned and said, "Be at my place at eight Saturday night. I like steak. I want to see a great movie and I won't fuck you."

"Good enough! Eight it is," Steven heralded as he put his Miami Vice swagger to the forefront once more.

Paris just shook her head as she headed for her car. Steven watched her as she drove away, then went back into his house and pulled up the files he'd just printed for Paris. "Man, what a nut case. Whoever is dating Abigail, I wish them luck."

Steven had failed to mention to Paris what he had seen along the way to the Abigail Long case folders. He sat down at his computer and re-hacked the facility. He began to see folders that contained obvious aliases like 'Goofy', 'Bugs Bunny', 'The Mule,' and 'Hound Dog.'

"Hound Dog?" he said to himself. "Let's see who the Hound Dog is." As the folder opened, he began to read what was in the file and whom the file was actually about. No aliases. "Holy moly!" he shouted as he backed out of the folder. Hurriedly leaving the site he saw a file called 'Maid Marion.' "Who the hell?" Steven clicked on the file and began to read. "Damn it!" he yelled as he immediately got out of the server.

Steven began a cleanup operation used by hackers to remove any evidence they were ever in a system. He hoped he had done it fast enough, as he caught himself sweating, something he was not used to doing after a hack.

Chapter 14

FREDERICKSBURG?

Back at Maggie's house, after everyone left the party, Jack, Wood, Lovey and Maggie went to the living room and sat down. Jack was seeing Maggie now in a light he couldn't wrap his head around. A killer? No way. "All circumstantial," he kept saying over in his mind. He seemed to be outside the reality of the moment.

Wood was loading the pipe he had retrieved from the tea kettle in the basement. Jack figured, "What the hell?" May as well get stoned and forget about it all. "It's bullshit," he told himself once more.

As the pipe went around the room, Lovey took a hit, then another, then stood up and walked to Jack and said in her Gilligan's Island "Lovey" voice, "Jack, dahling. Would you be so kind as to take this fucking pipe out of my hand?"

Wood exploded in laughter. Maggie giggled and Jack reached out and took the pipe as he came back down to reality. Everything was fine. Forget Paris and her detective work. "Everything is fine now," he said it to himself again as he hit the pipe. "Everything is fine."

Jack was taking his first long and deep hit when Maggie said, "We need to go to Fredericksburg." Jack blew the smoke out faster than he could handle and broke into a coughing fit. "Are you alright?" Maggie said, as she handed Jack her wine cooler. "Here, drink this."

Jack drank some of the wine cooler to cool his throat and

looked at Maggie. "Fredericksburg? Why do you want to go there?"

"Because that's where James Monroe is. Hel-lo? We've been talking about this for two days. Now that I'm cleared of the fire I can go."

"Don't you still have things to do here?" Jack asked. "I mean, your business just burned to shit and you need to go to the post office to get your mail forwarded. You also need to go to the bank to close your account, or at least change your business address and call UPS to tell them not to come. You have shit to do. You can't just up and leave." Then the most wonderful idea hit him. It was so obvious.

"Why don't Wood and I go to Virginia? We can check out where places are, set the stage for you and Lovey to come. It makes sense. You stay here. If we find anything, we'll save it for you. You're the catalyst in all this, not me and Wood."

Wood looked up from Jack's suggestion and said, "Hell yeah! Jack and me will go and scope it out. Real Hardy Boys shit."

"Lovey," Wood said, looking at his now quite stoned brick top girlfriend, "What do you think? You and Mags stay here, and we go to Virginia to see if there is anything for you two to come and see?"

Lovey went back into her Natalie Schafer voice again and said, "Oh, girl time. I just adore girl time."

Wood erupted again. "I love it when she does that. Man, it kills me!"

"So, it looks like we're headed to Virginia," Jack said looking at Wood. "Man, all this travel is rough."

Lovey looked at Maggie and said, "Girl time is good. We have places to go here, anyway."

Maggie got it. She was still shaken from her past life regression, but something was pushing her back down that road. With the guys gone to Virginia, she and Lovey could take their time with it. "You guys better not find James Monroe without me," Maggie said. "I got dibs!"

That night, Jack and Maggie went to bed already missing each other. It felt like they'd been together forever. Jack could still hear Paris tell him he was with someone who could be dangerous, yet at the moment he didn't care. She was intoxicating.

As he slipped into bed, Maggie lit a candle and said nothing. The glow of the flame lit the room in a warm light that could not have been more appropriate. Maggie then straddled Jack as her long dark hair fell down like a waterfall, frozen just before it reached the river below.

She leaned back and pulled off her shirt. Jack was looking up at his dream girl. When he closed his eyes, it was her that came to mind. She was both his lover and his fantasy. He reached up to her as she began to move in the candlelight.

"I was a naughty girl today. I guess I did something we should talk about."

"You were?" Jack responded. "I didn't see you being naughty at all. I thought you handled today admirably considering the circumstance."

"When you were out on the deck this afternoon, I took Sue down in the basement and made her come," Maggie whispered while studying Jack's face for a reaction.

Jack was lying there with Maggie on top of him. She was looking down and Jack was slightly startled at what she said. Now in unfamiliar territory all he could say was, "Oh, you did? You were naughty, weren't you?" He was sure she was just playing with his head. It was fantasy shit women tell their men sometimes to get them hard. Yet, her face was not revealing any sort of jest. It was a look of "I did it and I liked it!"

Maggie leaned down and began to recall how she and Sue spent those stolen minutes at the bottom of the stairs. Step by step, she relived it with him. With each whisper Jack became more and more turned on. Jack was beginning to leave the realm of playing fantasy and enter another phase in their lovemaking. His head was swimming in her detail. It was hypnotic. Maggie rose up and began to put him inside her. Jack was ready to feel her slide down on him, but she stayed there, suspended. Jack pushed upward only to have her pull away. She told Jack how Sue began to moan as she fingered her at the bottom of the stairs.

"She was coming, Jack. Sue was coming and I could feel her tightening as I finger-fucked her. I was fucking her, Jack. I loved it! Sue was coming!" Maggie then plunged down, taking all of him inside her. Gasping, she slowly moved up and down once, twice, and as she came down on him the third time, she stopped halfway, then back up, over and over. Jack began to twitch, move, and then close his eyes. Sensing Jack's climax she at last thrust herself down on him feeling him explode like a geyser inside her. Jack stayed hard until moments later she, too, let herself go in a crushing orgasm that left them both exhausted and looking into each other's eyes.

If this was a dangerous woman, Jack told himself at that moment that he was now choosing to live dangerously.

Wood and Jack's plane landed in the afternoon. Maggie had given them a list of places to start. The object of the road trip was to find Blanch's house, if it still stood at all, but the chance of a house from that era still standing alone in the woods was remote at best. During the Civil War over one hundred thousand soldiers were killed in battles within a twenty square mile radius of where they were going to try to find their needle. Buildings were either burned or suffered cannon attacks. The haystack was huge and they knew it going in. Maggie said they would need a map of Fredericksburg that was drawn from the 1700's and suggested the courthouse was a good place to start.

They arrived at the Fredericksburg, Virginia Courthouse at around 3:00 pm. Jack was the point man asking for directions as Wood tagged along like a little kid, curious, but quiet.

"These government places make me nervous," Wood admitted as he looked into the offices as they passed by them. "This is where it all goes down, man. I'm tellin' ya, they know all kinds of shit about us that we don't even think about."

Jack had to smile. "You really are stuck in the sixties, Wood. It's not as bad as you think. It's all mostly for security reasons. They want to see who's got what and what they plan to do with it, mostly. Get that?"

"I'll feel better when we're outta here," Wood admitted.

They came to an information desk with a lady behind it. Jack walked up to her and immediately turned on his salesman charm. "Hi, I'm Jack Reynolds. I'm looking for information about old structures from the 1700's specifically. Would you know of any such buildings in Fredericksburg?"

The lady looked up at Jack and Wood and said, "Sir we have many buildings from that era still standing. They are on the historical register. Would you like a tour guide? It has all our older buildings in it with a history of who built them. It's free. Take one if you like."

The lady pointed to a small stack of cheaply printed pamphlets with "Fredericksburg Historical Landmarks" on the front.

"Why, thank you!" Jack said as he took one.

He looked at Wood and said, "Perfect! We start here."

After leaving the building the two sat at a picnic table under a large tree outside the courthouse. Jack flipped through the pages of the book and said, "There are a lot of old houses here from the 1700's, but these are mostly downtown. It said in Blanch's ledger that he had to walk to town. He found James and Spence Monroe in the woods and killed James there. I don't think Blanch's house is anywhere near town."

"Wasn't there something about a waterfall?" Wood said. "Seems like Blanch's wife, Hope, was buried near a waterfall. Do waterfalls last two hundred years?"

Jack had to hand it to Wood. What he said made perfect

sense. There was a waterfall in the ledger and that would put them near a stream or river. The next move would be to find a wooded area near the closest river or stream. They knew nothing of the Rappahannock River and its miles of wooded shoreline at that time, but they were about to be educated.

Jack's phone rang and he looked down to see who it was. "Holiday" showed in the display. He didn't want Wood to know he was having Paris check up on Maggie, so he told Wood he needed to catch a work call. Wood took the opportunity to find a bathroom.

"Jack!" Paris said after his answer. "My guy did the hack on Abigail Long."

Seth could be heard in the background from the speaker, "She's dangerous Jack! Get away from her. She's psycho. It says in the files that Abigail Long was diagnosed with a multiple personality disorder. She has issues, Jack. One of her personalities is a man, it says here. The doctors put it in her file that when this man personality comes out, your girlfriend can become violent and is capable of homicide. Homicide, Jack!"

"She could kill you in your sleep, man," Seth said. "She wouldn't even know she was doing it. She would be someone else in her head. It's a big file. It says she has an I.Q. of 170. Smart lady. She has a photographic memory and she's been known to sleepwalk. You see her sleep walking any?"

Jack rationalized, "No, but we haven't been together that long."

"It says here one of her personalities suffers from nymphomania, which they say is common is cases like this. She is bi-sexual and does kinky shit. You see any of that, as if I want to know, ol' buddy?" Seth said with a suppressed chuckle.

"She's hot, yeah, but nothing out of the ordinary," Jack said as he told a lie. He remembered the night before and Maggie's description of how she brought Sue to a monster climax. She told him she was bi-sexual. That wouldn't be out of the ordinary. She wasn't hiding anything. He didn't know if her little fantasy scenario with Sue was the truth or just her playing sex games. "Can you send me the file? I'll read it on my own. I'm in Virginia for a few days with … an old buddy."

"Virginia?" Paris said. "You're not with Abigail Long? What's in Virginia, Jack?"

"I'm onto something here," Jack said. "No lie. I think I found out the fifth President of the United States wasn't who he is supposed be. We are re-writing history. Look, I gotta go. If you find out anything else send it to me. I really appreciate you two."

"What? Jack, are you all right? You're re-writing history now?" Paris said, with a hint of sarcasm in her voice. "People that try and re-write history usually end up being a part of history themselves." It was then Paris heard a tell-tell clicking noise on her phone. Hackers learn to listen for anything out of the ordinary when they are on the phone or online. It can mean someone else is listening in to the conversation.

"Don't worry about it. It's all in fun!" Jack said as another lie left his lips.

Paris then realized she needed to cover their conversation and said, "You and your detective hobby. You're always acting like you're doing some secret agent crap when you should be working. I'm glad you're having fun. Be careful out there. Talk later!" And Paris hung up.

Jack was a little taken aback by what Paris had just said. Wood was coming towards him from the restroom. "Let's go find a river," Wood said, ready to get away from the government facility.

Jack looked around and had to agree. He was still thinking about Maggie. That file had to be wrong. That's what he told himself anyway.

Back in Georgia, Paris had an uneasy feeling. Was someone just listening to her talk to Jack?

Maggie and Lovey were sitting on a pile of pillows in the middle of the floor facing one another holding each other's outstretched hands. Candles were flickering around them as the sun was setting on the Colorado mountains.

Maggie once more had the blindfold on and was only focusing on Lovey's voice. It was a voice that had guided many people into a place where they at first believed they could not go, and then stood corrected after they returned.

"We are going back to where you once lived in 1785. Let this world go. Travel in your mind back two hundred years to Fredericksburg, Virginia. You like it there. It's your home. You feel safe. Nothing scares you or would ever hurt you. Look around and you'll see old friends and family that love you. Sit quietly and feel where you are. Sit quietly."

Lovey watched Maggie and tried to sense whether or not she had become deeply enough entranced to travel back in time. There were no signs yet. No twitching, no swaying, just the cold hands of a woman who was daring once more to take a leap of faith to answer her own questions.

Lovey sat quietly for a few minutes, then asked Maggie, "Is it a nice day there? Is the sun shining?" Maggie suddenly opened her mouth like she was going to say something and froze. Lovey whispered, "You see your friend, Elizabeth, don't you? What is she wearing today?"

Still, Maggie seemed like she was on the verge of saying something. She dropped Lovey's hands. Lovey watched as Maggie's right hand began to clinch into a fist. Her eyes began to twitch as if she was in deep REM sleep.

Lovey leaned in and whispered, "Are you with Elizabeth? Who are you with?"

Then Maggie's arm flew back with her fist clinched. She lunged at Lovey stabbing at her with an empty fist yelling, "Kill you! Kill you! Kill you!! Beth is my wife gon' be! I……kill…..you!"

Lovey was on her back holding Maggie's fist in the air. Lovey began to scream, "Wake up! Wake up! Wake the fuck up, Maggie!"

Maggie pushed Lovey's hand away and went for her throat. Lovey felt her hands tighten around her, as she suddenly couldn't breathe. She was trying to scream "Maggie!" to no avail. She looked to her right and saw a glass filled with one of Maggie's wine coolers. Lovey's long arm barely reached it. Clutching the wine cooler, she threw the cold liquid into Maggie's face. Maggie recoiled and released her grip on Lovey's throat. Lovey reached up and pulled the blindfold off of Maggie and slapped her as hard as she could across the face. Maggie fell backwards in the floor and lay there gasping for air.

Lovey rolled over and tried to see if Maggie was back to herself. Maggie opened her eyes, then raised her hand to her face to feel the cold wine cooler all over her.

"Maggie! Say something!" Lovey said on the verge of hitting her again.

Maggie's eyes began to grow wide as she looked around the room. "Lovey? Where am…..I was there. Damn it, I was there! Oh, God! I killed him. I killed James Monroe! I saw it as well as if I were just there."

She looked down at her wet shirt and said, "How did I get wet?" Then, she looked at Lovey, who was obviously shaken. "My God, what happened to you?"

Lovey now realized Maggie was herself again and breathed a sigh of relief. "You damned near killed me! I had to throw that cooler in your face to get you off of me. What were you seeing?"

"I saw Monroe. It was him. I was actually with James Monroe! I ran into him on the road. I killed him with a stake I was going to use to hold down a beaver trap down by the river. There was someone else I couldn't quite make out. He saw me kill Monroe and ran away. It must have been Spence. He called him 'Jimmy.' I think it was Spence Monroe, the twin. Yes, it was! It was him! He ran away before I could get to him. My God, Lovey, it's true. The ledger is true! The real James Monroe died at the hand of Daniel Blanch, my ancestor. I saw it all happen. It's true."

Lovey was still enjoying the fact that she was alive.

"I have done hundreds of these things but never, not once, has anyone gone ape shit crazy on me like you did."

As she picked her tall frame up off the floor she staggered to a chair. "I need a hit." She reached over to the coffee table, picked up Wood's pipe and put it to her mouth. She lit the lighter and the flame descended into the bowl as tiny billows of smoke began to emerge from it. Lovey sat the pipe down and then fell back in the chair. As she exhaled, she said, "We can't do that again. No fucking way. It's too dangerous. You've tapped into something far more deeply than anything I have ever seen anyone experience. If I hadn't gotten to that wine cooler, I'd be dead now. I'm not kidding, Maggie, you were gone. I mean, you were Daniel Blanch!"

"I could see the path in the woods," Maggie reflected. "It was more of an old road, really, with lots of trees. I could hear water running. It sounded like a river was running by the road. I saw Monroe and went after him with a stake. He went down and I stood over him and looked up to see Spence running away."

"How did you know it was Spence? Was he Monroe's identical twin?" Lovey asked, now starting to forgive Maggie for her sore neck. "Were they identical?"

"I don't know. I just knew it was him," Maggie said as she strained to remember details that were evading her.

"What about the notebook?" Lovey asked. "Did you see the notebook? It says in the ledger that Blanch took the notebook from Monroe and hid it somewhere. If we knew what it looked like, we'd know what to look for."

"I didn't see it," Maggie said closing her eyes. "I saw Spence run down the road and that's when I came out of the trance."

Lovey got up and went to the ledger. She opened it and held it as far away from her as she could, like she was trying not to get infected by whatever disease it carried. She turned the pages and began re-reading the text that Blanch had written:

> *"I done went and tok the man who tok my Elizbeth from me and I made him ded. His nam was Jimy Monro. His dobl brother I herd him cal Spenc run off or Ida kilt him to. I kilt Monro with stob I whitled. Now my Elizbeth wil be with me. I hav the notbok he wrot her love leters in I tok from his pokit. My Elizbeth wont nevr see non of them. I hid it here and nobody gon no."*

"I wish I knew where 'here' was," Lovey said. "If we had that notebook it would.....wait a minute. He said, 'I hid it here.' You don't think...."

Lovey looked up at Maggie and began to let her hands run around the cover of the ledger. It was large and padded. Maggie came over and together they felt its thickness.

"Oh my God! It can't be this simple. Get a knife."

Lovey sat the ledger down on the countertop and Maggie got a butcher knife. Maggie surgically began to cut across the top of the backside of the ledger. As she pulled it apart, multiple pages were revealed. "I think it's here!" Maggie shouted, getting excited.

"Be careful, go slow," Lovey instructed, as she watched Maggie slide the cover off the ledger. As Maggie slowly pulled up the pages from the back cover, a forgotten notebook saw the light of day.

"This is it!" Maggie said, in an excited whisper. She laid it on the counter and read the words aloud: Office of the Governor Thomas Jefferson, Virginia, 1782.

"Oh my God!" Maggie said as she sat down. "This is it." She slowly turned the pages to reveal well ink and quill handwriting. There were notes, dates and even a grocery list.

Lovey stared at the notebook that now consumed Maggie.

"It says 'Thomas Jefferson.' I thought we were looking for James Monroe."

Maggie took a deep breath.

"It makes perfect sense. James Monroe was a prodigy of

Jefferson's. Jefferson was Monroe's mentor. This notebook originally came from Jefferson's office, so Monroe probably picked it up while he was there."

Lovey was getting anxious.

"See if you find anything in there about Spence."

"Lovey, darlin' slow down. Let's take this in. We have just uncovered something that should, by all accounts, be in a museum. It's a personal effect of the fifth President of The United States. We can't just go flipping through it like it's a grocery store tabloid, for cryin' out loud. Let's take a minute here. Besides, James Monroe's father was named 'Spence'."

There were faint ink lines that seemed more art than manuscript. The swirling letters in the faded ink held a beauty for Maggie that was unexplainable. Her history studies had all referenced documents like this, but she never thought she'd actually be holding one.

"It's beautiful!" Maggie whispered as she turned the pages. She began to read:

> *September 18th, 1782*
> *I have the honor of being elected to the House*
> *of Delegates. I thank Thomas for the good word*
> *he spread on my behalf. I am the youngest man*
> *in the House and pledge to do well and not*
> *disappoint T.J. He is truly a great man.*

"Holy shit, the man is talking about Thomas Jefferson like he's a neighbor or something. Can you imagine?"

> *"They don't respect me at all. These men see*
> *me as a spy or just someone put here to tell on*
> *them and their dealings with the Army. They*
> *walk away from me when I approach like I am a*
> *turncoat. They call me 'boy' and laugh when I*
> *speak out of place. I am learning, but these men*
> *have no respect for me when I tell them the*
> *government should have the right to regulate*
> *the commerce of merchants and trade for the*

benefit of the people and the government. I am met with most uncertain stares and whispers upon my insistence of such issues."

Lovey was curious. "What does that mean?"

"It's history," Maggie explained, still looking down at the notebook. "I never knew Monroe was looked down on while in office. It makes sense if you think about it. A young guy, twenty-two at the time, being put in with a bunch of old stuck-in-their-ways farts? I feel his pain." Then Maggie jumped at the sight of a word. "Spence! Here's Spence!" She began to read:

> *"I met Spence today to discuss the talks. He has been invaluable to me. Remember to discuss Treaty meeting. What was said?*
>
> *I wish I were more like him. He has the passion to stand up to them I don't possess. Our charade is working. They are respecting me more now each time I see them."*

"That's it!" Maggie yelled. "Lovey that's it. He's using Spence to stand up for himself!"

"You mean his brother has balls and James doesn't?" Lovey suggested.

"Looks like it," Maggie agreed as she continued reading random passages.

> *"Elizabeth was well today. She looks fair and proper in her dress. She and Spence talk and laugh. I watch them from the carriage. Our parents would be proud of her. She has dealt with the death of Captain Kortright with admiration. She is a good person and a fine sister to both Spence and me."*

"Sister!" Maggie exclaimed. "Elizabeth was their sister. That explains it. That's how Spence was able to marry her, she was his own sister, and nobody knew. When Blanch killed James, Spence just slid in and took over, then went on as James all the way to the White House. Spence and Elizabeth were in love. Not James and Elizabeth."

"That's gross!" Lovey said. "He married his own sister?"

"It wasn't that uncommon, Lovey. In those days it happened more than people realize. There were few records on anyone. It was wartime. People got shuffled all over the place. That explains why she didn't want Blanch around. She was a widow to a Captain Kortright and that let her change her name from Monroe so nobody knew. Lovey, this is the smoking gun! This proves that James Monroe had a twin that married his own sister after James was killed. Do you realize the implications here? It could potentially make the entire Monroe presidency a lie. The Monroe Doctrine, the acquisition of Florida, states being ushered into the union. It all could potentially be ruled invalid."

"It sounds big, but the real smoking gun is Monroe's body. If the guys can find that, with what we have here, we really can re-write history. But Maggie, I have to ask you, do we really want to? I mean the guy has been dead now for two hundred years. He's been credited with a lot of stuff. Why tarnish all that? I don't get it. Why go to all this trouble?"

Maggie then turned and looked at Lovey as her eyes began to twitch and roll. She looked as though she were about to faint, then she lunged forward at Lovey and screamed, "Because he stole my Elizabeth from me! I kilt him dead with a stob and I still lost her to that double! That double brother! She was mine!"

Lovey fell back on the floor and looked up in horror as Maggie's face contorted to an evil stare. Every pore in Lovey's body became saturated with a fear she'd never known. Then, as suddenly as it had happened, Maggie's eyes rolled back and she fainted behind the counter.

Lovey sat there not knowing what to think or do. She slowly got up, saw the butcher knife on the table and grabbed the handle. She peered around the corner to see

Maggie lying on the floor, unconscious from the outrage she'd just exhibited.

Lovey stared down at Maggie, not sure if she should wake her. The phone rang and startled Lovey once more. She let out a shriek as the first ring blared through the intense moment. Lovey dove for the phone and answered it. "Wood? Wood is that you?"

Wood and Jack had found the Rappahannock River. The question of whether or not there were still woods next to it had been answered. The river had a fine example of a wooded shoreline that went on for miles. Wood heard Lovey and picked up on her anxiety-laden answer.

"Lovey? Yeah it's me....."

Lovey cut Wood off mid-sentence.

"Wood there's something wrong with Maggie. We found the notebook! It was in the back of the ledger's cover. Maggie read it and we found out it's all true and then she turned into Blanch and ...and..."

"Lovey! What's goin' on there? Slow down."

Jack was standing next to Wood and got a sense of his conversation. "What the hell is it? Is something wrong?"

Wood was still trying to make out what was happening.

"Calm down. Just take a deep breath and tell me what's goin' on. Breathe."

Lovey, still watching the unconscious Maggie, began to repeat herself as slowly as possible.

"Wood, we found Monroe's notebook."

Wood looked at Jack and said, "They found Monroe's notebook!"

"What?" Jack said, startled at the thought. "Where the hell...?"

"Wait," Wood said to Jack. "Hang on. Keep goin' Lovey."

Lovey explained, "We found the notebook in the ledger. It was in the back of the cover."

Wood excitedly turned to Jack.

"It was in the back of the ledger's cover!"

Jack shook his head at the thought of it. They'd had the notebook all along.

Lovey was speaking in a nervous whisper.

"Maggie was reading from it and just went crazy. She thought, or she was….Daniel Blanch!"

Just then, Maggie began to stir.

"I gotta go. She's waking up! Oh, shit! What do I do?"

Maggie woke up and looked around the kitchen floor where she'd found herself. "What happened?" she asked, as she looked up at Lovey still holding the butcher knife. "What am I doing on the floor?"

"Wood, it's okay, she's coming out of it. I'll call you back." Lovey hung up leaving Jack and Wood wanting to come home immediately.

Jack was dumbfounded. "What happened?"

"I don't know. Sounds like Lovey hypnotized Mags into thinking something weird about Blanch. She had a bad reaction to it."

"What kind of reaction?" Jack asked, now worried that these signs may be related to what Paris had warned him about.

Wood didn't want to alarm Jack and offered, "Oh, it's nothin'. There's nothing to worry about, let it go. Just crazy girl stuff."

Lovey walked around to where Maggie was lying.

"Are you alright?" she asked as she bent down to help Maggie up off the cold floor.

"I….I'm not sure. We were looking at the notebook and then I was on the floor. How did I get there and what are you doing with that knife?"

"You went weird on me, Mags. No shit, honey you were acting like you were Daniel Blanch and he wasn't happy."

"What!" Maggie said, as she came back more and more. "Blanch? Why do you say that? What makes you say that? What happened?"

"We were talking about Monroe. I asked why…." Then she stopped. Before, when she had brought up the Monroe secret, Maggie had gone all Blanch on her. She didn't want a repeat performance, to say the least.

"Why what?" Maggie questioned.

"Why don't we get up and get us a wine cooler?" Lovey answered. "I need a minute to think."

Chapter 15

THE BAIT GUY

Jack and Wood parked their rental car by the Rappahannock River. The waterfront was peaceful and still held the appearance it had been undisturbed, despite the civilization just a few minutes behind it. The phone call bothered Jack. Now, for the first time, he began to reference Paris's impromptu research on Maggie. She was in a mental hospital and now she was acting like she may need to go back. It was disturbing. He had to look closer at Maggie and try to see her in that light and that was hard for him.

"We need to call them back," Jack said, as he sat and looked at his phone.

"Lovey said she'd call. One thing about her, when she says she's….." Jack's phone rang and Wood said, "See? She's good for it."

Jack coolly answered the phone, "Hey! What's up! You alright?"

Lovey was on the other end. "We're fine. Mags just had a little moment here. That's all. She fainted at all the excitement of finding the notebook. She's fine now."

Jack didn't buy it. "You sure, or is she standing there about to do something crazy?"

Lovey laughed a half-true chuckle. "It's okay, really. We are back in this century now. How are you?"

Jack was listening for any sign of trouble and was trying to act naturally. It was then he heard the same clicks on his phone as before with Paris. He shook it and listened again. He assumed it was the bad reception from where he was.

"We are sitting by this river. Man, it's a major forest here. If that old house is still standing, it's going to be next to impossible to find."

Maggie was sitting at the counter looking at the notebook again. She motioned she wanted to talk to Jack. "Mags wants to talk to you. Here she is."

"I'm fine," Maggie assured as she took the phone. "I just fainted. Jack, we found the notebook. It was in the cover of the ledger the whole time. I know it sounds crazy, but it's true. We have proof that Spence Monroe took over as James. It's all here. If we can find James's body, we can re-write history."

"It was in the ledger the whole time? Unreal!" Jack said. "Anything in it about Blanch?"

"No, not that I've seen," Maggie continued. "We did find where Spence and James met and replayed meetings with Congress. It seems that Spence was more aggressive than James and had qualities that James didn't have. I guess Spence didn't take any shit."

"Shit from who?" Jack asked, now totally out of the loop.

Maggie told Jack, "It's a long story. I'll fill you in when you get back. I need to spend some more time with it."

"I want to see that notebook," Jack insisted. "Look, we are by the river. It's miles of wooded shoreline and I have no idea how to go on from here. A building still standing in the middle of all this is a long shot, Maggie. You may have to settle for just the notebook. You have the pamphlet in your safe deposit box. With that and the notebook, you could have quite a payday at auction. I say we just go with that. It's enough. We don't need Monroe's body."

Maggie then became agitated again for a moment.

"It's there goddamn it! It's there!" She then slammed the phone down.

Lovey jumped back and said, "Maggie! Stop."

As Maggie looked down at the phone she'd come close to breaking, she slowly put it back to her face.

"I'm sorry, Jack. I need to get some rest. I'm a little out of sorts here with all this."

"Good! Lie down." Jack insisted. "Take some time and get your shit together because you are scaring us here. All this will work itself out. Calm down. Now, let me talk to Lovey."

Maggie handed the phone to Lovey and didn't say a word. She knew he was right. There was something inside her that she felt but didn't understand. She needed time.

"Jack?" Lovey said. "We're fine here. Keep looking for the Blanch house, for a while at least. Maggie seems to need to know you're doing it. Remember, Blanch said he buried Hope near a waterfall. Find a waterfall and you may be close. I'll keep in touch."

"Take care of her, Lovey. She's scaring me."

"Me too!" Lovey agreed, trying to be comedic.

On the other end of the phone Jack caught the undercurrent in Lovey's voice. There was more going on than she could say and he was getting worried.

"You sure you're alright there?"

"Talk to you later!" Lovey answered, evading his question, and then hung up.

"Shit!" Jack said. "I don't like this. I don't like it at all."

He needed to know more about Maggie's mental state and wondered how much Wood knew about her stay in the psychiatric hospital. Surely, he had to know she was in there.

"Wood, has Maggie ever acted a little out of sorts before?" Jack began. "I mean, has she ever seen anyone professionally for anything? Some people see other people when they have problems. Has Maggie ever, that you know of now, seen a professional psychiatric doctor for anything?"

Wood shrugged, "You mean a shrink?"

Jack was walking on thin ice. "Yeah, but more involved."

Jack didn't want to pry, but he had to know if Wood knew Maggie had been institutionalized.

"Don't ask me. We keep in touch, but sometimes we go a while without talking. You know, little breaks in the parental advisory chats."

Curious, Jack asked, "How long was the longest break?"

"Oh, about three years," Wood recalled. "I was busy. So was she, I guess. We didn't have a fight or anything. I just went one way and she was at school. Why?"

There it was. It was entirely possible that Maggie could have gone into a facility and Wood not have known. But that still left one big door open he needed to close. Who was Abigail Long? If he asked Wood, then Wood would put together that Jack had help researching her. Then the trust factor would come into play. This was suddenly getting complicated. Jack decided to leave well enough alone for now. He and Wood were still faced with trying to find Blanch's house, if it still stood. Lovey was right about the waterfall. He needed to find someone who knew the river.

Jack studied their situation. "We need a guide."

Wood scratched his head.

"A guide? Like a river guide? Hell, we don't need a guide, we just need somebody who comes out here a lot. Like a fisherman. Some guy who fishes up and down the river."

Jack looked at Wood and said, "Wood, that's great! A fisherman. We need a bait shop. Surely where there's a river there is a bait shop. They would know the river."

Jack and Wood pulled out and headed back to the main road. A gas station was nearby and Jack, while filling up, asked an attendant where a bait shop was. He was directed to Almario's Bait and Tackle Shop just up the highway. After finding it, Jack told Wood to wait in the car. He heartily agreed. As Jack walked in the old bait store, an old man was behind the counter tying bait flies.

"Hello!" Jack said, as he pulled out his salesman charm. "I need some information about the river, and I was wondering if you could help me out. I'm Jack Reynolds."

Jack put out his hand and the old man shook it suspiciously. "I'm trying to find a waterfall near here. Not a big one, it could just be a stream's waterfall. Do you know of any like that?"

"Why do you ask?" The old guy replied. "There are a lot of places out there to put a waterfall. Big and small."

"I found an old letter one of my great-grandfathers wrote. He talked about having a house in this area, somewhere, near a waterfall. It wouldn't be a major waterfall, but one in a stream or creek. This was over two hundred years ago. I realize things change, but he had a stone house near it as well. It would be nothing but ruins now, I guess, but I'd still like to find it, you know? Just to see it. In the letter, he said he buried his wife there. That would be one of my great-grandmothers. I want to maybe mark the spot for family records. Maybe have a family get together there or something. Can you help me out?"

"I gotta say, I never would have figured you for that," the old man said. "Yeah, I know a place like that. It's a creek waterfall that runs twenty-five feet or so. Good drop. It's still there, but I can't vouch for anything that would have been near it two hundred years ago. Everything's changed, you do realize. We've had floods. Big ones. If your grandfather's house was near the river, it probably got washed away or buried by the mud. Like I said, a lot has happened in two hundred years."

Jack realized just what a long shot he faced. He had not even considered floods, which would have changed the entire landscape. Still, Jack was hopeful.

"Can you direct me to where you think the location may be?"

"I'll draw you a map. I wish you luck. It's a good thing you're doing." The old guy took a piece of paper from his printer and started to draw.

"It's a little ways off the dirt road that runs by the woods. Follow the map. It's a popular spot with folks. Real pretty. Lots of pictures get taken there."

Now, Jack and Wood at least had a solid place to start, even if finding the old Blanch house was a long shot.

Jack went back to the car and showed Wood the map.

"Good as shit! Now we're talkin'. We need to find that place and get back home. I don't know, I got a weird feeling about all this."

Jack agreed. "You and me both, brother," as they headed back to the river.

Chapter 16

HOPE BLANCH

Maggie had now settled into a wine cooler and Lovey began to get another dark feeling. She felt the ledger had a soul, but now it was apparent it wanted something far more than just to be read. It wanted blood. She had to find out more about it. The only place she knew to go was back to where its journey had begun, and that was the trunk where Jack and Maggie first found it. Maybe there was some detail or clue they overlooked. It was all she had, but she had to try.

"I need to go out for a bit, Mags. You need to rest. Take a nap. Go outside and let all this settle. I need to go talk to Pete and Sam because I haven't seen them in a long time. We have stuff to talk about. You know, same old shit."

Lovey pulled the Jeep into the parking lot of the now cold remains of the Antique Barn. She went to the out building and opened the door. The piles of old boxes lined the path to the back where the trunk still sat, now opened and plundered of its bounty.

Lovey saw the other books that she concluded were previously in the trunk, lying by its side. She picked each one up and ran her hands over them and felt nothing but cold. She turned her attention to the trunk itself, handmade and well crafted. She let her hands run over it and around its side fittings and hinges. Then, she got a jolt. She jumped back like something had just hit her mind from out of nowhere.

Lovey studied the frame and let her eyes wander into the bottom of the empty trunk. She put her hand in, and as it got closer to the bottom, Lovey felt a dark sense of urgency. Looking at the outside of the trunk, she noticed a discrepancy. There was more room. Several inches separated the bottom of the trunk from the dirty concrete. Lovey reached over, took the crowbar in hand and began to pry up the trunk's old bottom. As the boards came loose, she reached in and pulled them out. Looking down, she could see a leather envelope under the wood. Freeing the boards around it, she reached in and picked it up. A flood of images raced through her head as she held it for the first time. They were scenes of screaming women, lost and helpless as flames leaped around them. Lovey felt a sharp pain in her neck and had to drop the envelope and catch her breath.

She stared down at what she had found and then, slowly, picked it up like she was handling dynamite. Lovey untied the leather string that bound it. Inside was a stack of very old parchment pages. The first page read:

> *Executed in League with The Devil:*
> *Summons and Certificates of Death*
> *Fredericksburg, Virginia, 1801*
> *Witches and Warlocks*

Lovey read the first page. It was a summons written in well ink on parchment to a Rebecca Middlebrook. It said she was summoned to answer charges of devil worship and witchcraft. The next page was a certificate of her death with "Hanged as a Witch" written above a series of signatures. Lovey read page after page of summons and death certificates of women accused of witchcraft.

The last page in the envelope was what she was looking for; a connection to Maggie. She held it and read:

> *"Hope Blanch you are hereby summoned to the*
> *court of Fredericksburg to stand trial for*

*consorting with the Devil and using witchcraft
to spoil the crops of Bartholomew Campbell."*

The rest was unreadable.

"Hope Blanch!" Lovey said out loud.

The next page attached to it was a death certificate for Hope Blanch, hung as a witch in 1802. She was pronounced dead and buried as to her husband's wishes. The rest of the summons letter, however, was in scribbles. Lovey replaced the boards and closed the trunk, then headed back to Maggie's house with the envelope. Maggie needed to know what the entire summons letter of Hope Blanch said.

Chapter 17

AT THE FALLS

Jack and Wood precisely followed the map the bait man gave them. It was actually well drawn and led them to a parking spot where Jack pulled in. "Here we go," he announced as he got out of the car.

"After you," Wood gestured, as the two started down the path.

Soon, the sound of running water could be heard.

"I hear it," Jack said as they got closer. Then, as they rounded a bend in the path, there it was, like something out of a story.

"Bingo!" Wood shouted as they approached the picturesque waterfall. "This is it. Gotta be!" He began to look around at the obviously well traveled area.

Jack suggested, "We need to spread out and find the house."

Wood said, "I'll stay here a bit. I like it here. You look around and I'll be here."

Jack left Wood at the falls and began his search for any structure he could find. He tried to imagine what it must have been like back in the days of Daniel Blanch and James Monroe. It was probably much more wooded with a lot of scrub brush and vines two centuries ago. He was truly looking for a needle in a haystack. After a wide search he realized it was futile. Whatever was left of the Blanch home was long gone. He felt like he'd failed Maggie. He thought of her and how she wanted this so badly. It was all for nothing. No body, no proof of a changeling president. It all seemed so far-fetched now, he had to laugh.

When he returned, he found Wood sitting on a rock near the falls looking up into the falling water. He shook his head at the long shot they had taken, only to find nothing but scenery.

"No house!" Jack yelled out. "I looked all around and I can't find anything resembling a house at all."

"I didn't think you would!" Wood yelled, still sitting there in a curious pose. "I had to see for myself, though. I'm glad we came."

"Yeah. Better head back!" Jack yelled out over the sound of the running water. "At least we found the falls. Nice spot. No dead presidents though. You think we should wait to tell Maggie?"

Wood nodded. "Yeah. Let's tell her when we get back tomorrow."

"Tomorrow? You want to stay overnight?"

"Yeah, why not? I've never been here before, it's late, and I don't feel like getting on another plane today. Let's go back tomorrow morning."

Jack agreed. "Why not? I'm in no hurry to get back."

After a steak, the two found a couple of rooms at a cheap motel. As Jack was heading to his room, Wood said, "Hey! Give me the keys. I want to go for a drive for a bit." He held up his fingers to his mouth like he was smoking a joint. Jack laughed, threw him the keys and said, "Not me, I need a break."

"Suit yourself," Wood laughed as Jack turned to go into his room.

As Jack laid down to go to bed, he wanted to call Maggie but his phone was dead. He had forgotten his charger and just stared at the dead cell phone with all his numbers in it. He really missed Maggie. He so wanted to tell her he'd found Blanch's house so she could come out and they could together change history.

At one forty-five in the morning, Jack was sitting in a chair by the window and saw a car pulling in. When he glanced out to see who it was, he was surprised to see Wood getting out of the car and heading for his room. "What on Earth? That must have been a long joint!" He started to open the door and then decided to just leave the little guy alone. Maybe he got lucky and found a bar to hang out in. Who knew? Reluctantly, he got back in bed and tried to sleep.

The next morning Jack had to wake Wood up. He banged on his door at ten o'clock. When the door opened, Wood was standing there looking like hell.

"Long night?" Jack said slightly. He didn't want to give away that he saw Wood come in so late.

"Couldn't sleep. Went to a movie," Wood said in a growl.

"Movie? What movie?" Jack asked.

"The kind where the name or plot doesn't matter," Wood replied.

"Oh, THAT kind of movie," Jack acknowledged. "I see. When the mice are in Virginia they go see porn movies. Sounds like a bumper sticker."

"We need to go, I guess," Wood said as he shielded his eyes in the morning sun. "Gimme a minute."

Jack had to laugh. Wood managed to find a porn movie house in Virginia. Too funny! What made him laugh was that he wasn't surprised at all.

Jack and Wood got to the airport, returned the car and set the plan in motion to be back in Colorado by 6:00. Wood seemed quiet. Preoccupied even. Jack couldn't wait to see Maggie. The hours were hanging like days.

Chapter 18

LOVEY AND THE BIG BLOW

Maggie had gone to bed after a dose of "help" from the medicine cabinet. She missed the comfort of having someone else to hold as she'd gotten used to feeling Jack next to her. Lovey, on the other hand, was wide-awake. She had brought the summons envelope in from the car without Maggie's knowledge. There, in a back bedroom, she set it on a desk and brought a lamp over to see more clearly the swirling scribbles on the old parchment. She read aloud:

> *"Hope Blanch you are here by summoned to the court of Fredericksburg to stand trial for consorting with the Devil and using witchcraft to spoil the crops of Bartholomew Campbell."*

Lovey held the page up to the light trying to see through it. Still no clue as to what it said. She turned it upside down and began to see words appear that had been written upside down and backwards.

> *"If you read this aloud as you stand you will surely be burned as a witch. If you do not, then you will be hung for consorting with the Devil to damage the crops of Bartholomew Campbell."*

"What kind of crazy....?" Lovey said to herself. "It must have been a test to see if anyone could read it. If you did, then you got burned. If you didn't you just got hung by the neck." She then looked at the Death Certificate again and said, "You must not have read it right Hope. They hung you for it."

Lovey closed the book and lit a candle. She knew what she was doing was dangerous but had to know what lay beneath the energy she felt when she first found the envelope in the concealed bottom compartment of the trunk. After getting herself centered, she sat cross-legged in the middle of the bed, holding the summons envelope and letting her hands run across it as she felt its edges, its back, and the string that held it together. Lovey slowly began to pick up images of women screaming, sensing their pain as the visions of flames leaped around her. She took deep breaths trying to keep apart from the nightmarish images.

Lovey began to see gallows in front of her and could feel herself walking up the steps where a noose hung freely in the wind. She turned to see the blurred faces of people watching as she had the noose fitted over her neck, then turned to see the hangman's hand on the lever. She braced herself for what she knew was to come and just as the lever began to move from the hangman's strength, the door to her bedroom flung open and Maggie stood in the doorway screaming, "You bitch! What are you doing in my head? Get out! Get out!"

Maggie ran towards Lovey and flung herself onto the bed with outstretched hands.

Lovey shouted, "Maggie! What are you...?" Then Maggie's hands found Lovey's neck again. She was being choked once more. Falling back on the bed, gasping for air, she could feel her body beginning to go limp as the air left her lungs. From across the room she saw a blur of someone running towards them from the doorway and heard a thud. She felt Maggie's body fall on hers and then Lovey blacked out.

As Lovey began to come to, she looked at the clock. Almost half an hour had passed and Maggie was still on top of her. She rolled Maggie over and whispered, "Maggie?" Lovey moved off the bed and looked all around the room. The leather summons envelope, along with Hope Blanch's death certificate, were gone. She looked back at Maggie and reached over to put her head on a pillow. As she did, she noticed a red blood spot on the bedspread where Maggie's head had been. "What the hell?" She picked up Maggie's head and felt fresh blood on the back of it.

"Maggie!" Lovey yelled as she ran to the bathroom to get wet towels. The time was one forty in the morning. She didn't want to call anyone, but if Maggie couldn't get up, she may have to.

The wet compresses on Maggie's head seemed to help. At last she began to stir.

"Maggie! Mags darlin'!" Lovey said, looking for any sign of response. At last, Maggie began to moan. The sleeping pills she had taken had done their work. As Maggie came around, Lovey held her to her chest and began to talk softly.

Chapter 19

BACK TO MAGGIE MOUNTAIN

At last, when Jack and Wood were finally headed up the mountain back home, Jack said, "I was really into the James Monroe thing. Maggie will be disappointed. We have a ledger and a pamphlet. That's all. No body. No victim, no crime."

"It wasn't a wasted trip," Wood said. "I enjoyed it!"

Jack pulled into the driveway of Maggie's house and Lovey came out immediately. There was a look of panic about her. As Jack parked, Lovey ran to Wood's side of the car and opened the door.

"Maggie's hurt! Doc Collier just left."

"Hurt? How?" Wood and Jack both said at once.

"We had a visitor last night. Someone hit her over the head."

As the three went into the house, Lovey told them of how she was once more attacked by Maggie. Then she told of the figure she saw come from behind Maggie and hit her. Now, Maggie had a concussion from the blow to the head.

"She needs to be in a hospital but she won't go," Lovey said. "The doctor told her to stay in bed for a few days, but we all know she won't!"

Jack wanted to see Maggie. "Some vacation, I gotta tell you two. I have not been off of work for a week in years, and when I finally do take a vacation I end up in all this bizarre shit! Remind me not to take any more vacations."

Jack opened Maggie's door to her room to find her standing up and looking out the window.

"What are you doing up?" Lovey scolded. "The doctor told you stay in bed."

"What happened here, Mags?" Wood asked as he sat down beside her.

Jack went to Maggie and hugged her. "You are a handful I gotta tell you. You okay?"

Maggie tried to explain what happened but had very little recollection of anything. "I went to bed and woke up here with this headache. I wish I knew more, but I can't remember any of it. Lovey says I attacked her. What happened in Virginia? Did you find Monroe?"

Jack was studying Maggie's face.

"Hang on about Virginia. Why would somebody come in here and hit you on the head? It doesn't make sense. For someone to be here at the exact time you were supposedly attacking Lovey is too far fetched. There has to be more to all this."

He was again haunted by Paris's findings on Maggie's mental instability. Could this be why she was in the hospital to begin with? Moments of schizophrenia? Multiple personalities? He hated himself for it, but he found he was rethinking Maggie and why they were together. She was showing signs of instability that even he couldn't overlook.

Lovey told Wood to help her make something in the kitchen. Jack stayed with Maggie as Wood followed Lovey out.

As they left, Maggie turned to Jack and said, "So? What happened? Did you find the waterfall?"

Wanting to put his doubts about Maggie to rest, he replied, "We found what we think is the waterfall Blanch mentioned in the ledger. I looked all over the area. No house or any building at all was anywhere near it. A guy at a bait store told me there had been floods there over the years, as it is next to a river. Whatever happened to Blanch's house happened a long time ago. Between the Civil War battles and random acts of nature, I'm really sorry Maggie, it's just not there anymore."

Maggie was obviously disappointed. "I was so sure. I knew we'd find it. I just knew it!"

"Sorry darlin'. Not happening."

As Wood and Lovey cleared the earshot of Jack and Maggie, Wood turned and said, "What the fuck, Love? Why did this happen?"

Making sure they couldn't be heard, Lovey told Wood to sit down.

As they sat on the sofa, Lovey took a deep breath and said, "Wood, I found something out in the old trunk where Maggie and Jack found that ledger. I went back to see if there was anything else we were missing and I noticed there was a compartment in the bottom of the trunk. I removed some boards and found an old leather envelope. Very old, like the ledger. Its summons and death certificate records that were from the same time period. It was full of women who were either hung or burned in witch trials! I found documentation of Hope Blanch being hung as a witch. It had her summons and accusation letter in there. Whoever hit Maggie on the head stole it."

"Stole it?" Wood said alarmed. "Did anyone see you leave with the envelope and bring it here?"

"No. Not that I saw. I'm telling you, I came straight back here. I was reading it in my room when Maggie came running in screaming for me to get out of her head. It was bizarre. She started to choke me and as I was passing out, I saw.... someone. I couldn't make out who it was."

Chapter 20

PARIS AND THE LINCOLN

Paris had been uneasy since the hack on the hospital. She had information she couldn't stop reading. It was fascinating to her and each time she read the printout of the documents she found something else she had missed.

It was Saturday morning and the mountains of North Georgia spread out for her like a freshly painted picture as she sat on the deck of her small rented house near Ellijay. It was noon and the sound of the television was faintly heard while she was on her deck. Then, one name jumped out at her….The Snowman.

Paris turned to look at her television and saw her friend Steven being led out of his house in handcuffs by men in black. "Oh, shit!" she yelled, as she ran into the living room and turned up the sound. The anchorman was telling of how Steven Winters, AKA "The Snowman," was caught hacking a government facility in Virginia and making classified documents available online.

"What?" Paris gasped. "Government facility! I thought it was a fucking nut house!"

What had they stumbled into? Had she been the catalyst for her friend to go where he shouldn't be? What did the government have to do with any of it? She was just trying to help Jack, now here she was thinking she was on the verge of being charged with espionage. Paris grabbed the files The Snowman had gotten on Maggie and then left her house. As she drove through the mountains, she wanted to call Jack, but it was too risky. She knew that if someone were watching her, because of her working with The Snowman, then she'd be listened to everywhere there'd be an opportunity. Besides, she was already hearing suspicious clicks on her phone. She needed to get to Seth to tell him about Steven Winters (The Snowman) being arrested, if he didn't already know.

Paris was passing a roadside scenic overlook where she usually tried to stop whenever she could. As she drove by, she threw a glance over to the curb and saw a black Lincoln with dark windows. She looked in her rearview mirror to see the car pull out behind her, so she pressed down on the gas pedal to distance herself. Through the mountain turns the car stayed back, not approaching too close until Paris at last reached the factory where she worked. When she pulled up in the parking lot, she watched as the car slowly drove past her. Seth's SUV was parked on the side. She let out a sigh of relief and ran up to the door, which was curiously unlocked.

"It's Saturday. It shouldn't be unlocked," she thought as she opened the door.

As she walked in, she yelled out for Seth. Paris cautiously made her way back to the office where she had hoped to find him. He wasn't there, but his computer was turned on and a fresh pot of coffee was made. She went down the hall and noticed Jack's office door was slightly open. As she walked into the room, she froze at the sight of Seth sitting behind the desk with a bullet hole in his forehead. Paralyzed, she tried to scream but no sound came out. Fear had taken her from head to toe, as a single tear appeared to flow down her cheek. All her senses told her to run. Get out now! As she looked down at the file in her hand, she assumed that whoever did this knew she was involved with The Snowman, or did they? The car that just followed her to the factory had ample time to take her out on the mountain road. That hadn't happened. The right thing to do at that point was to act as naturally as possible. If she ran, then she'd be red-flagged as being part of the hack for sure. The right move was to call the police to report the murder.

She slowly backed out of the office doorway and went to her own office and called 911. When the phone rang the operator answered with, "911 emergency. What is the nature of your call?"

Paris took a deep breath and said, "I'd like to report a murder."

Hours later, Paris sat on the front steps of the factory and watched as Seth's covered body was rolled out into an ambulance. The local police had a real crime on their hands and were milking it for all it was worth. They'd broken out fingerprinting kits and crime fighting paraphernalia they seldom, if ever, got to use. The local newspaper's reporter almost had an erection at the opportunity to write some real news about a local wealthy factory owner murdered in his own office. This was good stuff, and everyone was on it.

Paris had told the story three times already about how she was in the area and stopped by the factory to simply use the bathroom, saw Seth's car, and went to the office to find him dead. Apparently, it was good detective work to have the one who reported the crime recite in detail how they found the body. Paris was annoyed and scared. She thought she had done well and done the right thing calling in the local authorities. It was then, as she finished her story, such as it was, for the third time that she noticed the black Lincoln in the parking lot at the end of the street. It looked out of place among the local Jeeps and four-wheel drive pick-ups that frequent the mountain town. She tried not to study it too closely. As the ambulance left with Seth inside, Paris asked the sheriff if she was through and could go back home. Actually, she had no inclination of going back home. She wanted to find some place safe.

As Paris turned to leave, she was met with the local media wanting quotes, pictures, anything to print to show that the Ellijay View newspaper was on the job. She simply said, "no comment." As she got in her car to leave, she noticed the Lincoln was gone. She slowly pulled out and headed in the opposite direction of her house.

She was driving on remote control. Paris had to call Jack but didn't want to use her phone. She stopped at a Quick Trip gas station down the street and called him from there. As the phone rang, she had a knot in her stomach.

Jack felt his phone vibrating in his pocket. He reached in and saw an unfamiliar number. He was going to close it and not answer but he realized the area code was from Ellijay, Georgia. His gut told him to answer it. He listened to his instincts and hit "answer."

"Hello?" Jack said as he wondered who the call was from.

"Jack! Oh, thank God!"

"Paris? What's wrong?"

"Jack, Seth's dead!"

What?" Jack yelled as he recoiled from Maggie.

"Seth got shot in the head at the factory. Somebody came in and killed him!"

"Paris, are you serious?"

"Hell, yes! It's all over the place up here. Listen, I can't explain why now, but I need you to call me back from another phone. I'm not shitting you. Call me back at this number from another phone. Don't use your cell phone."

"Okay," Jack assured her as he hung up his phone.

He went over and picked up Maggie's landline and she said, "What's going on?"

Jack began to dial and responded, "Remember the guy I was going to buy the ledger for? My boss who collects tools?"

Remembering the conversation Maggie responded, "Yeah, what about him?"

"He no longer collects tools," Jack said as he dialed Paris. "He was just found with a bullet in his head."

Jack heard the phone ring and a frantic Paris answered. "Jack, listen, I was being followed by a black Lincoln this morning. When I pulled into the factory, I came in and found him at your desk shot in the head. I've been talking to cops all morning. And something else, the guy we paid to hack the hospital where Abigail Long stayed was on the news this morning getting arrested for hacking a government facility in Virginia. Apparently that place was under government watchdogs. I think that place is a lot more than just a mental facility. I think people go there, or have been there, that nobody wants anyone knowing about. High up people. You getting me here, Jack?"

"Holy shit! Where are you?" Jack asked, trying to focus on all the drama just handed him.

"I'm at the Quick Trip down the street from the factory. Jack, chances are your phone is tapped. I was talking to The Snowman, his name is Steven Winters by the way, and then called you on the same phone. Be careful what you say. I got a bad feeling about all this. I think someone is onto you for something. Is there anything else you want to tell me about what's going on with you and why you went to Virginia?"

Jack's face went cold. He had been having conversations with Maggie on the phone about exposing a dead President as a changeling with his twin brother. The government is probably not going to be happy about that little bit of information.

"Whatever it was you said or did it struck a nerve here," Paris continued. "I guess they were listening to the conversation when I called you from the factory about Abigail Long, or Maggie Styles, or whatever you call that woman you're shacked up with. That's how they knew to come here, and..... oh my God! Seth was shot in your office at your desk. Whoever did this was probably looking for you! They came in and Seth was in your office at your desk for some reason. Your name is on your desk on the nameplate. They came in and saw Seth and thought it was you!"

Jack's ear was going numb. "Paris, slow down and who the hell is The Snowman?"

"Oh, for cryin' out loud, Jack! He's the guy who hacked the hospital looking for info on Abigail Long. He was just arrested for it. Aren't you listening?"

"If the hacker was arrested for it, then why would they come in and shoot Seth, thinking it's me and then just arrest the hacker? The Snowman is the hacker. Not Holiday....or me. Why would they let The Snowman live if this is so bad?"

"I have no idea, but we need to talk. Are you coming back to Georgia any time soon, I hope?" Paris asked as she was plotting her next move. "The Snowman taps will eventually lead whoever this is back to me. If they don't know I'm involved yet, they will soon enough. Then they'll come after me."

An idea just came to Jack. Paris was an excellent hacker and very resourceful. She was a target in Georgia, so why not bring her to Colorado? He held is breath and then said it. "Paris, you need to come to Colorado. Go to the airport now. We can get whatever you need here."

"What? Jack, I can't go to Colorado. Seth has just been killed! Did you hear me! I have to deal with the business. I'm the only one who knows shit. Customers will be calling, relatives. This is a mess! I gotta deal with it here first. Are you coming back for his funeral?"

Funeral? Jack hadn't had time to think of a funeral. Seth was his best friend as well as being his employer. The family would probably want him to be a part of the service somehow. Then an interesting fact occurred to him.

"Paris, if they missed me once, like you said, what makes you think they won't try again if I come back?"

"Holy shit. That's right. Chances are, they know you are alive. They missed you and got Seth. It's all over the place down here. You need to lay low. Don't use your credit cards. It'll be an easy trace to you. When was the last time you used one?"

Jack remembered the trip back from Virginia and the motel room there. "I've been using it a lot lately."

"Did you use it in Virginia? That's where the hospital is.'

Jack realized he'd gotten a motel for him and Wood in Virginia. "Yeah, I got a motel there."

"Jack, that puts you near the hack site. Chances are someone is already onto you. You need to be careful. If they traced you to Colorado then you've been targeted. Has anyone odd been around lately?"

Jack looked at Maggie, Wood and Lovey and said, "You have no idea. Paris, you've got to come to Colorado. I need you here. The factory will be a crime scene for a few days at least. The local PD will probably bring in some detectives from Atlanta to look things over. You don't need to be there. Just get in your car and drive to Charlie Brown Airport. It's a couple of hours away. I'll call a friend of mine who has a plane and I'll get him to fly you out here. I'll pay for it. He owes me so it'll be cool. No passenger manifest, no credit card. Just do it Paris. I'm serious. I need you here."

"Jack, if I run to Colorado they will know."

"Nobody will know. You go to the airport and find Mike Conway. I'll call him. He's always flyin' somewhere. He has a nice plane that'll get you here under the radar."

"You sure about this?" Paris said in an uncertain tone.

"Yes, damn it! Come to the Denver airport. I'll pick you up and explain everything on the way here."

"Okay, I'll come. I've got to go now. Stay off your cell phone. As a matter of fact, take the battery out of it now. They can triangulate you by finding your phone."

"Done." Jack said as Paris hung up.

Chapter 21

FREAKIN' STEVEN

Steven Winters, AKA "The Snowman," was taken into a small room after a long drive to Atlanta. He was being charged with Federal computer hacking, which was no small offense. He naturally had his "I'm not sayin' shit!" attitude on, but when three Feds walked into his room with a disc that had a couple of gigs of incriminating data against him, his attitude began to change.

"Hello Steven. I'm Bill Cantrell. These are detectives Sloan and Baker. You've been busy. We had you on our watch list for quite awhile, but your latest escapade into the Bowden facility in Virginia tipped your scales. So, you want to tell us why you went after files on Abigail Long?"

Steven sat there not saying anything. He had rehearsed this moment in his mind that if he ever got caught what his posture and response would be. Oddly, all that preparation was slowly going out the window. Having three Feds staring at you in a room makes you see things differently.

"Look, I want a lawyer. I'm not saying a word until I get a lawyer."

"You can have a lawyer if you want, you can sit there like a rock, or, we can let you go," Detective Cantrell said.

Suddenly magic words were ringing in Steven's ear. The "let you go" part was resonating and he liked how it sounded.

"I like the 'letting go' part of that. What's it going to take to make that happen?"

"Tell us who hired you to hack Bowden. Who wanted the

files on Abigail Long?" Cantrell said frankly, "We know you're The Snowman. We know more than you think about your little world of computer Superheroes. The fact of the matter is we let you do what you do so we can watch. You hack them, and then we hack you so we don't get traced. It's that simple. We don't need to watch anyone directly anymore. We just let you little hack monsters rummage through the computers we want and we just soak up what you find."

Steven was suddenly insulted. "What do you mean you hacked me? Nobody hacks me! I have the firewall that Moses couldn't part. Don't tell me you've hacked me. I'd know."

"Steven, who do you think we are? We aren't the U.S. Government. We're worse. They contract us to do dirty work for them. That makes us invisible and dangerous to people like you. We can hack anybody. That's how it works these days. Detective Baker here is one our chief computer techs and has something he wants to show you."

Detective Baker looked younger than Steven and he felt an immediate hacker dislike towards him. Not because he's hooked up with Feds, but in the hacker world the top of the hill is a sharp point and that position was The Snowman's, not this college guy in a tie with glasses that looked like they were windshields from a fifty-five Chevy.

Detective Baker turned the laptop around towards Steven and put in a DVD with a little cartoon snowman on it he drew. "That's you," he said as he smiled and slid in the disc.

Steven said, "What is this? Game time? Please. I left my controller at home."

The files began to unzip. Steven looked at the screen and saw files from his shadow drive.

"Look familiar? This is from your shadow drive, Snow dude. The one not supposed to be on your system? If we can hack that, how easy is it for me to get through to the rest of the easy, and I did say easy stuff?" Detective Baker glowed in his revelation.

Steven was now behind in the game. He realized Baker was good. Very good. There were files on the shadow drive that could put Steven in jail. Not the little jails, but the Mack daddy places they film 'Lost In Jail Hell' movies about.

"You must be proud of yourself. If I had all your hardware I could do that, but you need to realize, I get into places with one thing that you don't have and that's the reality that if I get caught, I could end up where I am now. By the way, where did you go to high school?"

"High school? Why?" Baker asked.

"Just curious. Where? I'll show you a trick of the trade."

He then turned to Detective Cantrell and said, "Where did dickless here go to high school?"

Cantrell looked at Baker and said, "Where did you go to high school?"

"Washington High School in Delaware," Baker answered reluctantly.

"Watch," Steven said as he took the laptop.

Baker protested but Cantrell held his hand up.

"About what, 2005?" Steven assumed.

"'06, thank you." Baker sneered.

Steven's fingers began to fly at the keyboard. As Steven landed, he pondered for an instant and then, "Yeah, oh that's good."

Baker had to protest. "What is this? You are letting this guy have access to our system."

Cantrell just held up his hand and in two minutes Steven said, "Here you go. Great likeness!" He turned the laptop around and on the screen was a picture of Baker from high school taken from the Computer Club group shot. His head was cut off and pasted on a picture of Dorothy from The Wizard Of Oz.

Baker's eyes grew wide in despise and Cantrell and Sloan busted out laughing.

Baker was pissed. "You think this is funny, Snowfucker? You want to play games here?"

"No, I don't want to play games, I just wanted to see you in a dress." He then began to snicker.

Cantrell asked calmly, "Detective Baker, why don't you leave us for a minute."

"What? Why? I want this guy." Baker protested.

"I'm flattered, but you're not my type," Steven said calmly.

Baker left with a door slam and Steven was left with Cantrell and Sloan.

"Okay, I get it. You're the cool smart detective Cantrell; Baker is the so-called tech guy who is standing on the other side of that glass right there with his arms folded and about to bite a hunk out of the wall. That leaves you, Detective Sloan. You must be Psyche Profile. You're trying to establish my state of awareness of the situation and whether or not I mean what I say or not. If this was Star Trek: Next Generation, you'd be a hot Betazoid named Deanna, Baker would be Wesley Crusher and Cantrell would be bald! Am I close?"

"Dead on," Sloan said. "Personally, I liked the original Trek better."

"So how am I doing? Looks like you might need to reserve some couch time for Detective Baker. He seems a bit pissed off," Steven said glancing a smile to the window.

"We obviously let you do that," Sloan admitted. "You know that. It was a little fun at our colleague's expense to put you in an imaginary driver's seat for a minute or two. It helps me profile you, but you know that as well."

"Yeah. I know that. How am I doing?" Steven sighed.

"Well, by the fact you threw a little digital tantrum there, I'd say you were a guy who's high school experience sucked, you were singled out as a nerd, you knew you had abilities but just wouldn't use them in the right places. You probably hacked your fellow student's homework and played hell with it. Girls were a problem for you, so you lived out your jollies online in porn houses where you hid your identity and then went as far as to hack the stars themselves trying to dig deeper into a kink that you think you created on your own. By the way you put Baker in that dress tells me you visited transsexual sites and liked what you saw. Now here you are with a God complex and you don't even know half the shit we have on you. Am I getting warm or do we want to talk about your childhood? I'll have fun with that one." Sloan turned to the window and said, "Detective Baker? You feeling better now?"

"You were right about the porn sites," Steven agreed as if nothing were wrong at all. "Your mother looked really good on hers."

Sloan's brow then began to tighten. "You little shit don't even mention my mother in the same sentence as the filth you…"

"Ho! He shoots, he scores!" Steven heralded in triumph. "Look who can dish it out but can't take it? Detective Sloan, momma's boy of the psyche squad!"

"Hold on you two!" Cantrell said as he stepped in. "We do have an agenda here and it's not name calling each other's mothers, for crying out loud. Detective Sloan I'll handle it from here."

Detective Sloan looked as pissed off as did Detective Baker. He left the room with the same door slam as Baker's.

"Well that leaves us, doesn't it?" Cantrell said.

"Yep. Poetic isn't it?" Steven responded.

Cantrell walked over and sat on the desk and said, "Steven we have a problem. I'm done playing so I'm just going to spell it out."

Steven figured he knew what was coming. He wasn't going to say a word and then the unexpected came from Cantrell.

"Mr. Snowman, I want to offer you a job."

Steven looked up and said, "A job? What kind of job? Ratting people out?"

Cantrell was smooth. "We are prepared to offer you one hundred thousand dollars for your help. It's a one-time offer. It won't come again."

Steven looked up at Cantrell. "You're not serious. A hundred grand for what?"

Cantrell leaned forward. "You have the ability to hack places that aren't hackable by most people, that includes some of us."

Steven turned to the glass and said, "Hear that, Baker?"

Cantrell got up off the table and began to walk slowly around the room. "We have resources, but we don't want the traces coming back to us. We want to pay you to hack certain people and then get caught."

"Get caught? Why get caught? I thought the object of the hack game was not to get caught," Steven questioned.

"Because we need a fall guy. A digital fall guy who will go in, get us what we need and then get back out, leaving a few digital crumbs for those people to follow. They find you and come for you. We then intercept them before they get to you. All you have to do is..."

Steven interrupted Cantrell with, "Be the bait."

Cantrell looked at Steven and said, "Yeah. Be the bait."

"So, who is the hack? Maybe some third world country going after a nuke site? If you think I want Arabs coming after me you're crazy. I enjoy what I do but government shit is crazy hard to infiltrate. I can do it, but I'm not going after Arabs."

"You'd be working under strict guard. We'd be watching you twenty-four seven. When they come for you, and they will, we intercept them. They go with us and you get a hundred grand then go away to our site in Hawaii for a while. It's a safe house of sorts. You'll live there for six months and then come back to the states."

"A hundred grand and six months in Hawaii. This has nothing to do with Abigail Long?"

"It has everything to do with Abigail Long. I want to show you a picture. You have been in contact with a Margaret Frances. 'Paris' is her nickname. She uses the alias 'Cody' and contacted you about hacking the Abigail Long files. We know this so don't deny it."

"Wait, if you're trying to get me to say who hired me to hack Bowden that was a nice try but you have got to do better than that." Steven said as if he'd scored another point, or at least a block in the game he found himself in.

"She works for Holiday Cabins in Ellijay when she's not playing with you little hackers online," Cantrell said. "This picture was taken this morning of her boss, Seth Holiday. He's looked better."

Cantrell handed Steven the photo. Seth Holiday was as Paris found him, slumped over in a chair with a bullet hole in his forehead.

"This was taken when?" Steven said.

"This morning. It's all the rage in Ellijay. You see, Steven, we didn't bring you here to arrest you and charge you with doing naughty things online. We brought you here to save you from having a bullet hole of your own. We think you were the next target."

Steven sat there in a state of disbelief. "Hand me your cell phone. Does it work in here?"

"Probably. Why?" Cantrell said.

"Go to the Ellijay newspaper. I want to see the front page. It'll be out now," Steven said.

"Go there yourself. There's a laptop in front of you," Cantrell said as he motioned toward the laptop on the table.

"Please. Fake sites are nothing to pull off with a laptop. Doing it with your phone is another matter."

"Suit yourself," Cantrell said as he handed Steven the cell phone.

Steven then activated Cantrell's Internet and went to the newspaper front page and there was the headline, "Local Businessman Shot." He went to another site and there it was again, "Ellijay Man Murdered." He handed the phone back to Cantrell and said, "Shit. Okay, what now? What has this got to do with Abigail Long?"

"Somebody is hunting her and her boyfriend, Jack Reynolds. We think the bullet Holiday took was meant for Reynolds. We think he stumbled onto something with

Abigail Long that was never supposed to be seen by anyone. We just don't know what. We have an idea from some taps we did, but it's too insane to even comprehend the ramifications. We want you to go back and hack Bowden again. This time put some files in the folders that we tell you to, addresses, names, little stuff, leave a trail easy to find, then wait. That's it."

"That's it? A one time in and out for a hundred grand and six months on the island?" Steven said.

"Yeah, that's it. That, and we want you to kill Paris Frances."

"What?" Steven said standing up. "I'm no killer! I can't and won't kill anyone! I'm a hacker sure, but hey man, I don't even own a gun!"

"We know that. We checked. What, did you think it would be easy? We just hand you a hundred grand and then it's vacation time? You have to earn it, Snowman. Kill Paris and you're a free man," Cantrell said as he took a cigarette out of his front pocket.

Steven was shocked. "Why Paris? She didn't do anything."

"She got you to hack the facility. She knows things that are dangerous to certain people way up the chain. It deals with shit you can't imagine."

Steven was cautious. "Paris? I don't believe it."

"She's with Jack Reynolds right now. If they let out what they are looking for there will be hell to pay. We don't want that."

"Wait a minute. Who are you people? Who are you and what's going on with me killing Paris?"

"We are the people offering you a door out of this shit you're in. If I were you, I'd take it. Paris is dangerous. Think of her as a car. Jack Reynolds is driving that car and to us and a few other people, Jack Reynolds is dangerous."

"Who the hell is Jack Reynolds? I thought he was just some guy who sold cabins with Paris," Steven recalled, still standing now in a corner.

"Paris and Jack are close. We know this. She will use

whatever means she has to help Reynolds. We can't just tell her to stop. She won't. Paris Frances is Jack Reynolds and Abigail Longs', or Maggie Styles as she is called today, way of getting into places that will help them expose things. She's their own personal hacker superhero."

"Paris is good, yeah, but not that good," Steven said.

"She's good enough. With them together they can do our clients a lot of harm. We don't want that. Take out Paris and you're on Easy Street for a while. Don't, and it's you doing the Bubba Tango inside for the next ten years at least, or until your asshole wears out. Your call."

"Look, if she's that dangerous and Jack Reynolds is working with Abigail Long then why don't you just send a drone over where they are and blow them away yourself? Surely you can do this."

"Oh, sure. We could take them out, but we don't know who else is involved. We need to take out the eyes of Jack Reynolds and Abigail Long and those eyes are attached to Paris Frances. Great name, by the way."

Steven was stumped. He had looked into files that had cartoon names on them that held information on people high up. That info, if it got out, would be harmful to those in the folders. The agents had said nothing about his opening them. Now he had a decision to make. He needed leverage and he was betting that the folders would be it.

There was something else. He knew he was being played but wasn't sure to what extent. It occurred to him that there was probably no other organization looking for Jack and that Cantrell's people were the ones who killed Seth Holiday. It was all to make Steven think that there was indeed someone else in the game. He just wasn't buying it.

"Well, you leave me no choice. I guess I'm now a hit man for hire. Where is Paris now?" Steven asked, trying to see daylight again.

"She is in Colorado with Jack. A pilot we own is posing as a Mike Conway. He took her in Conway's personal airplane. We think that soon she will be headed to

Fredericksburg with Jack. That's where you need to do her." Cantrell said.

"A pilot you own. Man, this is some real movie stuff here. Where's the real Conway?" Steven asked, now sitting back down.

"We will fly you in, point you to her and then you pick the time and place." Cantrell lit another cigarette. "There will be a Glock in the glove compartment of the car we'll fix you up with. After you do her, text the number we give you, put the gun back in the glove compartment, drive to the location we text you and you're using sun block for the next six months in the land of lobsters and cheap hookers. A hundred grand should cover at least part of that in your case."

"What kind of car?" Steven said.

"What do you mean what kind of car? The kind we give you. Why?"

"I want a Ferrari," Steven said.

"A Ferrari? Are you out of your mind? We are not in the car business. This is no game. You do this or you're inside for ten," Cantrell established.

"If I'm going to be a hit man, I want to look like a hit man. You set me up with a Ferrari 599, the Glock, half the hundred grand up front and the beach, Paris is as good as dead. I'll even save you a plane ticket and drive to Virginia. Deal?" Steven said trying to seem in control.

Cantrell leaned back in his chair and said, "Okay, we'll do the car, you do the girl and it's deal on. You don't do the girl after us setting you up and you better start looking for a drone of your own coming to blow your hacker ass out of the imaginary world you're in."

Cantrell then handed Steven a flash drive.

"The hacks we want you to do are on here. Do those first and wait. If you survive the night, Paris is dead real soon."

"What if nobody comes for me?" Steven said. "What if I hack the sites and nothing happens?"

"Oh, it'll happen. You just sit tight and don't go near any windows."

"Great!" Steven said. "It's gonna be a long night."

"Oh, by the way, the pilot? Mike Conway?" Cantrell reminded Steven. "He's dead. We'll be in touch, Snowman."

With that, Agent Bill Cantrell walked out, leaving Steven in a freakin' state of mind.

Chapter 22

KIND OLD CAT LADY

Maggie, Wood and Lovey had just heard half of the conversation Jack had with Paris and were looking at each other like it was the end of the world.

"What on earth is going on?" Lovey asked immediately.

Jack shook his head.

"My boss died. Someone shot him and a friend of mine who works for us thinks I was the target, not him."

"You?" Wood asked. "What did you do to deserve getting shot?"

None of them knew of the hack on Abigail Long or the arrest of The Snowman.

"It's going to take a minute. I need to catch you up on some things." He looked at Maggie and said, "You too. Take a seat."

Jack then explained how he had told Seth and Paris about how crazy he was about Maggie. Paris did an Internet search on her and found out she used to be Abigail Long before she changed her name to Maggie Styles. Paris then hacked University records in Tennessee and ended up trying to hack the Bowden Facility after she found out Abigail Long had four murder charges against her. When she couldn't get through their firewall, she hired The Snowman. That's when the shit hit the fan. Jack assured them he had nothing to do with it. In the crossfire of the hack, Paris talked to Jack on her cell phone, which had gotten tapped as a result of her conversations with The Snowman after watchdogs flagged him after the Bowden hack. Someone tapped Jack's phone as a result of his association with Paris and accidentally overheard conversations Jack had with Maggie about exposing James Monroe as a changeling President.

"What did you expect to find out about me, Jack?" Maggie demanded as she sat and glared at him.

"I didn't expect to find out anything about you. I had no idea Seth would tell Paris to hack the hospital. None! Why would I? They did it on their own. Now Seth's on a slab and Paris is scared to death. I'm here wondering if I'm a target."

Wood was all about it.

"It's the government listening to us. I'm telling you! They are probably listening to us now!"

"Look," Jack began as he looked at Maggie, "You have to admit that what they found out about you is damned weird." Then he said the obvious. "Okay, now for the big question, Abigail, who is Maggie Styles?"

Lovey had to laugh.

"Maggie Styles was a name Wood came up with when he opened the Antiques Barn. He thought people would trust an old woman who sold antiques. He was going to put a logo together of an old lady in a rocking chair named Maggie Styles who was this kind old cat lady that lived up here in the mountains. In true Wood fashion he never did. He just told people it was named for his daughter and that was all anyone ever asked about it. That is until Maggie, or Abby as Wood once called her, decided to come up here and buy the business when she left the hospital in Fredericksburg. Maggie had been through a shit storm with the murder trials, so she just changed identities and wanted all of it behind her. Abigail Long was erased and Maggie Styles, who people already thought was Wood's daughter, moved in and took up a new life here on the mountain. Before she came, Maggie Styles was just a name on a sign. Abigail Long had her name legally changed to Maggie Styles. And now you know."

"What about the hospital?" Jack asked. Then he looked at Maggie, "Why'd you go?"

"It was the stress of the trial," she admitted. "I wanted to get my head straight and needed some care. I went there and it took a little longer than expected to get my head screwed on right."

Jack took a breath and asked, "What about multiple personalities? You were diagnosed with a multiple personality disorder at the hospital. Did you know that?"

"Who have you been talking to? Nobody knows any of that except doctors." Maggie countered, now on the offensive, "Who are you? Are you a cop or an investigator or something still trying to convict me of the murders? Are you a journalist?"

"No! I'm a freakin' cabin salesman from Georgia! I'm harmless. I just have very resourceful friends who want the best for me, one of which took a bullet this morning because he was at my desk back in Ellijay. The other one is on her way here now to try and help me sort through this mess. Her name is Paris and she's good at finding shit out, as you now well know. I need her here. I think someone is coming after her because she and another guy, The Snowman, hacked the hospital computers and got your records. He was on the news back in Georgia for being arrested for it. People we know have stumbled into something that has ruffled a lot of feathers. I don't think you realize it, but we are an inch away from having a SWAT team come busting in here. We need answers and Paris can help with that."

"Where does that leave us?" Maggie said coldly.

Jack looked at Maggie as Wood and Lovey looked on. "Maggie, or Abigail, or who ever you are, I felt a connection with you the first time we met. I walked into your life just as you did mine and I never looked back. These last days have meant more to me than I can tell you. Now I have a sense of purpose. That purpose is being with you through whatever this craziness we're in turns out to be. If you have issues, then I'll do what I can to help you through them. If looking for the body of James Monroe has triggered some black ops thing against us, then I'm in it as deep as you are, but I have a feeling it would be in our best interest to get out of here for a while. Together. And you can make whatever you want out of all that. I'm not going anywhere except with you."

"Good answer!" Wood said. "I think we need to go see Grace. She'll hide us out for a while. She's good for it."

Lovey nodded and then Maggie said, "Okay, it's settled. We will go see Grace and wait for that Paris chick to come up. Then what?"

"I have no clue," Jack laughed. "I'm not used to bein' in this kind of drama."

Wood and Lovey got up to go pack some things and Maggie and Jack sat there staring at each other.

"Thank you, Jack Reynolds, prefabricated cabin salesman from Ellijay, Georgia. A lot of men would be gone by now, but here you are," Maggie said taking Jack's hand.

"A lot of men wouldn't be sitting across the room looking at you either," Jack said remembering all he'd been through since they met. "They'd be long gone."

Maggie and Jack fell into each other in a scene that would rival Bogie and Bacall. They were together. As together as any two people had ever been, yet they both secretly wondered for how long. At that moment neither of them cared about any of it. They were just enjoying a damn good kiss.

Chapter 23

THE HIDEOUT

Wood, Maggie, Jack and Lovey walked into the Grizzly Beer like a pack of outlaws in from the range.

"Well now, here's a sight!" Grace called out from behind the bar. "What brings a rag tag bunch like you in here? Pull up a seat, or four."

Wood went up to Grace with a look in his eye of need.

"Grace, we're in some real shit. Can you get hold of Pete and see if he'll let us stay at his cabin?"

"What kind of shit you in? Maggie was cleared of the fire."

"It's more than that," Lovey said convincingly. "Jack here has some people after him and Maggie is…well…not feelin' so good."

Grace looked at Maggie and agreed. Something was up. She made a call to Pete and soon they were in his cabin out on an overlook that let them see who was coming up the long and narrow road.

"Great place huh?" Wood said as he surveyed the view. "I haven't been up here in years. This place is cool. No one is going to find us here. Pete's got to have some weed stashed somewhere in here."

Jack agreed. "John Dillinger himself would be proud to call this place a hideout."

Jack left the three at the cabin and started the journey to

Denver to get Paris. It was a welcome drive in solitude as he tried to sift through all that had been thrown at him in the last four days. His life had gone from simple to totally unpredictable and in a way he welcomed it. Jack thought back to his state of being a salesman, and then Seth came to mind. He finally, for the first time, had a moment to reflect on his friend. They had done a lot together over the years, now he was gone. Jack still couldn't believe it.

"Sorry man. I had no idea all this would come back home."

When Jack reached the Denver airport, he went inside the terminal and paged Paris Conway. 'Conway' was not her last name, it was the last name of the pilot, Mike Conway, who Jack was hoping he could see to thank for flying Paris. Shortly, a woman in a baseball cap and dark sunglasses came walking up to him.

"Jack!" Paris threw her arms around him.

"Hey! Paris thanks for coming. Where's Mike?" Jack asked as he looked around for his friend.

"He left," Paris said looking back. "He said you two were even and he wanted to get back, so he refueled and left."

"He just left? I don't get it. That's not like him."

Jack and Paris got in the car and they began their trip back. They finally had a chance to catch up.

"Jack, it was horrid. A black Lincoln was following me so I went to the factory. The door was open; I went in and called out to Seth. I walked around and saw your office open. I walk in and there he was with a bullet...."

Paris broke down and started to cry. Jack reached out to her in sympathy but was powerless to do much more.

"I'm so sorry, darlin'. I hate it that you found him like that."

"The cops were actually cool about it," Paris said as she wiped away her tears. "Usually cops can suck but they took my info three times, then just let me go. I went down the street and called you and here we are. What the hell did you go to Virginia for? I think there is something there you know about that other people don't like. You want to explain it?"

"Virginia," Jack said with a sigh. "Okay, you ready for this? I went over to an Antiques Barn that was across the street from a bar I spent the night in to see about getting Seth a birthday present. I was looking for old tools for his collection. I meet Maggie Styles...."

Paris jumped in and said, "Who is actually Abigail Long, murder suspect with great boobs."

"That's her!" Jack said, now excited. "We went to an old trunk that had an old saw under it. I opened the trunk and we found a ledger that's two hundred years old. It belonged to a guy named Daniel Blanch. Turns out, are you ready for this?"

"I'm just foaming at the mouth," Paris said sarcastically.

"We found evidence in this two hundred year old ledger that this guy murdered James Monroe, the fifth President of the United States, and James's twin brother, Spence, took his place and married his sister, who was Elizabeth Kortright. He then went on to be President using James Monroe's name! The fifth President of the U.S. was a changeling. He wasn't the real James Monroe."

Paris looked at Jack like he'd lost his mind. "What on earth?"

"I know! It gets better! Turns out that in the ledger this guy Daniel Blanch describes in detail where he hid the body. He walled the fucker up in a wall in his house and had to live with the stench of him."

"Ewwww! You're kidding me, I know," Paris cringed.

"We, me and Maggie's, I mean Abigail's father, whose name is Wood, short for Woodstock, left Maggie, I mean Abigail and Lovey, whose real name is Audrey, we call her Lovey because she talks like the Lovey on Gilligan's Island, went to Virginia to try and find the old house down by the river that a bait guy gave us a map to. We found the falls but there was no house, so we came back to Colorado. When we got back, Maggie, I mean Abigail, had been hit on the head by someone we don't know who."

"Why'd she get hit on the head?" Paris asked.

"She was strangling Lovey because Maggie thought she was Daniel Blanch!"

Paris sat there like she'd just been hit with a WTF bomb. Her head was spinning.

"Damn Jack! You came up here to sell a cabin and now you're playin' name games with crazy people! I had no idea! Take me back to the airport. Whatever is waiting for me back home has got to make more sense than all this."

"No, think about it! We have a shot at changing history. History! So, we decided to try."

"And you went to Virginia to try and find the two-hundred-year-old body of James Monroe in a house by some falls, you said?"

"Yeah, the ledger said Daniel Blanch, who is Maggie's ancestor, by the way, buried his wife who was hung as a witch by some falls near the house because the cemetery wouldn't take her. She supposedly put a whammy on this guy Bart Campbell's crops."

"Take me home," Paris demanded. "This shit is too crazy even for you. Do know how you sound? You sound like a crazy person yourself! Witches now, Jack? Fuckin' witches?"

"It was two hundred years ago! People got hung for being witches. It happened. This guy Daniel Blanch had a wife who was hung as a witch. Her name was Hope. They buried her by a waterfall near the stone house they lived in, which isn't there any more because of the floods. There were a lot of floods back then."

"You talked about all this on the phone?" Paris said catching her breath.

"Yeah, I must have said some of it on the phone. Why?"

"Because it all makes sense now. They think they've found the craziest person alive and they want to clone you to be President! Has to be!" Paris leaned her head back and started to laugh.

Now frustrated, Jack said, "Damn it! I'm in deep with this! I have proof! I have the ledger that we found. There was even a pamphlet with it that was written by James Monroe over some shit before the Missouri Compromise. I'm serious! Maggie put it in a safe deposit box. We have a notebook written by Monroe that Lovey found in the back of the ledger. It has details of Monroe's dealings with Congress and even Thomas Jefferson. They were buds, you know."

"This is all real interesting about James Monroe. I'll give you that. Now let's go back to the part where Maggie, or Abigail attacks somebody? Lovey you said? From Gilligan's Island?"

"We call her that because when she gets stoned she does this dead on impersonation of Lovey, Natalie Schafer from Gilligan's Island."

"While she's stoned?" Paris asked.

"Yeah. It's funny as hell."

"There we go! Now we're making sense. You've been smokin' some crazy ass weed! That's gotta be it. These people got you baked and now you're seein' shit. Wake up. Smell the coffee. This is all nonsense. It can't be true. It's too weird even for you!"

"Ok, I admit hearing it all at once has got to sound crazy. I'll agree. Even I can't believe it. But one thing's for sure, who ever heard me talking on the phone to Maggie about all this thinks I struck a nerve. We think somebody burned down Maggie's Antique Barn because of it. I don't know why yet, but something tells me it was because of the ledger we found there."

"Someone burned her place down? When was that?" Paris asked sharply.

"Day before yesterday. We got in, drove up, and there it was fried to the ground. It was ruled an accidental wiring thing, but it's all too coincidental."

"So why am I here? I thought you wanted me to help you out of something and now I see that you are the one that needs to be in a mental hospital!" Paris nervously looked out the window at the surrounding mountains.

"I'll show you the ledger when we get back to the others. We are staying in a cabin, by the way. The house is too risky for now. You said so yourself."

"A cabin? As in a cabin like our cabins we sell? With how many people? Five? Not counting Ginger and the Professor of course. Jesus! This just keeps getting better!"

Chapter 24

MY CONFIDANT AND FRIEND

Wood had at last found Pete's stash and was rolling a joint. Maggie was stretched out on the sofa and Lovey was out on the deck in one of her meditative yoga positions when Pete walked in.

"You folks look comfy. Got into a pickle, I hear."

"Pete! Hey! Just in time. I found some of the green in the sugar bowl. Sit down, you won't believe the shit we're in," Wood said as he put the final twists on his joint.

Lovey heard her brother come in and got up to go see him. As she walked in, Pete threw her a glance and said, "Audrey."

Lovey feigned a smile and offered a, "Hello little brother."

Maggie stirred back to life and said, "I can't get used to people calling Lovey 'Audrey'. I know its family and all, but she's been Lovey for so long, I can't call her anything but that."

Pete took a chair at the table. "What's all this about? Not like you to talk on the phone, Wood. What'd you say got you holed up here?"

"It's in the ledger," Lovey said. She got up and walked to the ledger, picked it up and took it to Pete. "I'll try and explain this." She read and pointed out the phrases pertaining to Monroe and how someone must have overheard what was happening. "They killed Jack's boss thinking they were killing Jack," Lovey said as she sat down.

Pete seemed to have a weird reaction to seeing the ledger.

"Maggie, are you sure they killed the guy because they thought he was Jack?" Pete began, seemingly playing detective. "Maybe your boss was into something that you don't know about. He could have been banging someone's wife or something and then the jealous husband gives him a bullet. There are a million reasons for it, but you think there is some black ops mission headed your way. It doesn't gel. There has to be more to it."

Maggie was still nursing her head. She rolled over and said, "This is serious, Pete. Jack knew the guy who was killed very well. His name was Seth Holiday. Mr. Holiday had some super hacker get files on me. The place they hacked was watched by someone and Holiday didn't know it."

"Get files on you? What kind of files? From Bowden?" Pete asked, now getting curious.

"Yeah. Apparently that place is watched big time," Maggie confirmed, rolling her eyes.

"How did that Holiday guy know about Bowden?" Pete asked. "I thought you buried all that shit with Abigail Long."

"I did. I didn't count on Jack's boss getting nosy and asking a couple of hackers to go in and get my files."

"Hackers go into the institution files and find out who you were before you came up here. The hackers then call Jack and tell him who Abigail Long was and why she was at the facility," Pete said as he reconstructed events. "Then, somehow Jack's boss takes a bullet, and now one of the hackers is coming here?"

"She's someone Jack works with. Jack thinks she can help us get out of all this mess."

"If she helps you out of all this then God love her for it. You folks are into some crazy stuff that I'm not even sure I believe or not. You can hole up here for a couple of days, but after that you gotta go. I'm hunting this weekend and need the cabin," Pete said as he got up to leave. "I think that

Presidential crap you found in that ledger has more meat than the Bowden hack. I bet someone likes our presidential history as it is and that's why they are coming after you, if anyone is at all. I'd quit trying to dig up the past if I were you folks. Look where it's gotten you so far."

As Pete turned to leave, the three of them looked at each other and knew he was probably right. Dead presidents? Re-writing history? What were they thinking?

Pete walked out the front door of his cabin to see Jack and Paris pulling up. As Jack opened the car door he said, "Hello Pete. Thanks for letting us stay here a bit."

Not saying anything, Pete walked on by and got in his truck. Paris got out of the car, inspected the scenery and said, "How nice. A real cabin for a change."

Before they entered the front door, Jack looked at Paris and said, "Hey, do me a favor, will you?"

"What? Another one besides being here?" Paris said in anticipation of what was to come.

"Yeah. Will you like her? For me? Throw out all the research crap, all the prep you did on her. Just say hello and try to like her, because Paris, I do. I really do."

Paris saw the sincerity in his eyes. He was gone over this woman. She was a mystery to Paris, but if Jack liked her that much then there had to be more to her.

"Okay. I'll like her, Jack. I'll like her."

As they walked into the cabin, Paris scanned the room and her eyes landed on Maggie. There she was, like some picture from a celebrity magazine. She had been researching the woman for days, now here she was in the flesh. Paris didn't know how to react. "Like her" kept ringing in her head, so she smiled.

Jack said, "We made it! You guys, meet Paris Frances. My confidant and friend."

Wood stood up and said, "Hot dog! The Calvary is here! I sure hope you're as good as Jack says you are. Call me 'Wood.' Everybody does. This is my girlfriend, Lovey, and that's my daughter, Maggie. You want to smoke a joint?"

Paris looked at Jack and winked.

"I'll pass on the joint for now." Then she turned to Maggie, smiled and said, "So, the famous Maggie Styles," and extended her hand to shake it.

Maggie sat frozen on the sofa looking at the fresh-faced Paris and said calmly, "You must think I'm a monster."

Paris stopped short and said, "What? No! I don't think you're a monster at all."

"Bullshit!" Maggie snapped. "You hacked my files at Bowden to show Jack what a crazy bitch I am and then you drove in from Denver with him while he obviously prepped you on my state at the moment. Now here I am in the flesh. I'm Maggie Styles, alias Abigail Long, accused killer. I'm the mental patient who has taken the man you obviously are in love with away from you like a thief in the night. And you want to shake my hand? Please!"

"Maggie!" Lovey barked. "What's wrong with you? She is here to help us. You apologize to her right now!"

Jack was dumbfounded. He'd just seen a new side of her. He was gone for the day and now she was acting like a totally different person. Lovey put her arm around Maggie, picked her up and escorted her to the bedroom.

Jack and Wood sat there stone-faced. "What got into her?" Wood asked.

Jack said, "I have no idea, but if this is a result of the knock on the head then we got to get her to see somebody."

Paris was shocked as well. She didn't know how to react to the lashing she had received from Maggie. She sat down by the table and asked, "So, can I have a look at the infamous ledger that started this mess?"

Jack got the ledger and gave it to Paris.

"Wow. This is old. Looks real enough."

As she opened the front to the first few pages the images of the old tools that Jack had spoken of came into light. As she studied them, a tear ran down her face and then she started to cry. Jack looked at her and immediately got it. Seth.

"He would have dug the book, huh?" Jack said in an understatement.

"Oh, man," Paris said wiping away tears. "He would have been all over this. I can see why you thought it would be something he'd like. I can't believe he's gone."

Paris let her hands feel her way around the old ledger now with a considerably thinner back since the removal of Monroe's notebook. "Where is the part about the murder?"

"It's in the back." Jack reached over and turned the pages for her. "See here? It's a little hard to read."

Paris put the ledger in the light.

"This ink seems a different shade here. It almost looks like it was written after some of this. The aging doesn't seem to match." Then she began to read each passage Blanch wrote.

"Holy shit, Jack. I can see where you'd think something like this would be for real. Do you have a magnifying glass?" Paris said as she studied the script.

"I have one," Lovey said. "I'll get it." Lovey returned with the glass, Paris laid the ledger flat and began to read the texts in more detail. As the glass moved up and down the pages, Wood, Lovey and Jack just looked at each other and shrugged.

"You say that Blanch buried Hope by a waterfall?" Paris said.

"Yeah. Wood and I went there. It's still there and people go there a lot it seems. I looked all around but floods must have wiped away all traces of any houses or anything."

"Yeah, we were there. Nice place," Wood added. "I looked around, too, but Jack's right. There's nothing left."

Paris sat and studied the script with the magnifying glass.

"I took a course in calligraphy in school once. They showed us all kinds of artistic writing and one of the most common mistakes people made was distinguishing the 't' from the 'l.' You say it says 'waterfall'. If you look here, there is a slight line barely visible. I think it says 'waterfalt' with a 't' not an 'l.'

"But 'fault is spelled with a 'u' in it," Lovey commented.

"Look at Blanch's spelling. It's shit! He can barely write,

much less spell. I think he said 'waterfalt.' Now what would that be?" Paris said looking up at the others.

Jack scratched his head. "A lake or pond maybe? A fault in geography is like a crack in the crust of the earth that earthquakes happen on. A 'waterfalt' might be something like that filled with water?"

Wood asked, "Yeah, I can see that. But would they call it that two hundred years ago?"

Jack got up, began to pace and said, "When Maggie read me the first few pages of the book, Blanch talked about powering a saw the way we power a bicycle, with pedal and chain power. He was ahead of his time, as bikes weren't built until much later. Maybe he's doing it again here."

Paris said, "We need a map of the area. Ponds, lakes, anything that resembles a reservoir. It could be a park or a recreational area."

Wood said, "Wait a minute! Jack, that lady at the tourist information place in Fredericksburg gave us a little magazine thing with shit in it from the 1700's. Maybe it has parks in it."

"Wood, you never cease to amaze me. I'll get it. It's in my suitcase," Jack said, as he went for the bedroom.

"Are you sure it says waterfalt and not waterfall?" Lovey asked again.

"Looks like it to me," Paris observed, still looking at the writing through the glass.

As Jack went into the bedroom and got the pamphlet, Maggie was laying on the bed staring at the ceiling. Jack stopped to say, "Hey! I think we got a break in the case. Paris thinks Blanch lived near a pond or lake or something. She says the 'l' is really a 't' in waterfall. It really says 'waterfault'. You want to come out and see?"

Maggie lay there with her hands folded on her chest and then turned to look at Jack with a painful stare. Jack froze at the sight of her. She slowly spoke and said, "The man that done took my Elizabeth is in the wall o' my mortar place. She's mine and he stole her from me!"

Jack backed up against the wall and confronted the voice. Maggie's beauty was distorted with the glare that came from deep within her. A cold chill ran all over Jack. He remembered the doctor's analysis of schizophrenia but stuck to the mission at hand and said, "Where is Hope? Where did you bury Hope, your wife?"

Maggie kept her stare and said, "By the water. There's a marker with her. Facedown."

Lovey came into the room and looked at Maggie and Jack. She gasped when she saw Maggie's face. "My God, she's..."

Jack held up his hand and silenced her. "Where is the marker? Where is Hope's marker, Blanch? Where is it?"

Wood and Paris slowly came into the room to see Maggie's eyes glare at them. "Where is Hope?" Jack asked, regaining her attention.

"She is with her marker. It's facedown. They won't burn her now. Her rock is face down so she can see I done it for her." Maggie continued.

Wood freaked. "Jesus, she's whacked! Is she a vampire?"

"Shhhh!" Jack said as he knelt down beside her. "Daniel Blanch, Hope wants us with her. Where is she? Where do we go to find her marker?"

Maggie's eyes grew wide and evil. Paris was mesmerized. She couldn't move or say anything. Never had any of them seen the likes of this.

Maggie said slowly, "At the waterfault where the sun sets first in the evening. She likes.....it.....there." Maggie's eyes closed and she was asleep. The four stood staring at her, not knowing what to say. Finally, Wood broke the silence.

"I gotta go!" Wood disappeared into the bathroom and the rest looked at each other.

"Have you ever seen that before?" Jack asked, looking at Lovey.

"Hell no! I've seen a lot of stuff but not like that. It's the goddamned ledger! I told you it was evil, Jack. I told you it was. We have to burn it. Now!" Lovey turned to get the ledger.

"No!" Jack yelled as he followed her into the kitchen. "That ledger is the only thing we have to find Hope. He wants us to find Hope. Don't you see? His house was near where Hope is. It's by the water where the sun sets first. Blanch said that. Its gotta be a place in front of a mountain range, or hill or something that shields the sun as it sets. We need to find that place."

"For what reason, Jack?" Lovey snapped. "Where is this going? Didn't you see her face in there? It was evil, Jack. Pure evil!"

"It was Maggie," Jack reminded Lovey. "Don't you get it? If we destroy the ledger, we may never get her back! We need it. It's all we have of Blanch's."

"I..." Lovey turned to face Jack. "I...I'm just scared." She fell into Jack and started to cry. "This is all my fault. I never should have opened the door. I never should have. Now sweet Maggie is full of that evil thing and it's all because of me. I should have listened to myself."

"Maggie is a big girl," Jack reminded her. "She knew there were risks. It's not your fault. It's mine. I found the ledger, not her."

Jack glanced over at Paris and gave her the pamphlet. "That's it."

Wood came out of the bathroom looking peaked.

"I've never seen eyes like that. I'm rollin' one now! Anybody with me?"

Paris was going through the pamphlet and said, "There isn't a lot here on parks, just old houses from the 1700's. Wait! There's a wedding section!"

"A wedding section?" Wood remarked. "You getting married is not what's goin' on here darlin'."

"No, people get married by scenic places like lakes, ponds, waterfalls and such. Here! There are three lakes listed for weddings. There is Fawn Lake; it's on a golf course. There's Lake Anna; it's huge. The last one is the Fredericksburg Reservoir."

"Where is that?" Jack asked.

"It's not far from town. Here is a picture," Paris said as she held up the picture to Jack who was still holding Lovey.

"It has hills around it. Maybe that's it! How big is it?" Jack asked.

"Not very. The river is not far from there. There are probably lakes and ponds all over the place," Paris supposed.

"That's it," Jack said coldly.

"Why do you think that's the one?" Wood asked, as he put the finishing twists on his joint.

"Because the pamphlet was given to us in Fredericksburg. I'm going with that," Jack confirmed.

"So now what?" Paris asked. "Are we trying to find the body of James Monroe or are we looking for the house of Hope Blanch? I'm seeing this as one and the same. Maggie is channeling Blanch, who's spouting off facts about where we believe the house is that contains the remains of Monroe. Is that right? We believe Monroe is where Hope lived? Are we just riding that wave to get to Monroe?"

Jack was sympathetic. "Daniel Blanch was a complicated guy. Obviously. Since we found the ledger, Maggie did a regression with Lovey and saw through his eyes. Now she can't seem to get rid of him. We need to go back to Virginia to end this because that's what Blanch seems to want. If we find where Hope lived with Blanch, Monroe should be there in a wall somewhere. I know it sounds crazy, but that's where we are."

Paris shook her head. "So, are we really going to Virginia?"

"Damn straight we are!" Wood said. "That's my kid in there. If some old dead guy wants us to find his house, then I'm there. Enough said."

Paris looked at Jack and said, "We gotta do this under the radar. There are people out there who are onto us, Jack. If we get close they'll, well, you saw what they did to Seth."

"When do we go?" Lovey asked now rising up to the situation. "When do we go end this crazy…."

"Go where?" was suddenly heard from the bedroom doorway. Maggie was standing there, looking peaked and holding the back of her head. "My head's killing me! I think I may have a concussion. Where are we going?"

"Maggie!" Lovey said as she walked over to her. "Are you back? Is it you?"

Maggie looked around the room, pointed to the refrigerator and said, "Do we have a wine cooler left?"

A sigh of relief went around the room. Jack walked over to her and hugged her. "You gave us a scare, kiddo."

"I did? What kind of scare?"

"The kind you don't want to have happen more than once in your life." Wood said. "You almost gave me a heart attack!"

"I don't understand," Maggie sighed as she slowly walked into the room.

As Lovey sat down next to Maggie, she began to tell her how she channeled Daniel Blanch. Maggie was apprehensive at first, then went with it as everyone backed Lovey up.

Jack told her, "We are leaving for Virginia in the morning. I want this over with."

Paris was apprehensive. "It's two days to get there by car, Jack. That's a long way."

"Screw it. We'll fly," Jack said.

"We can't fly! We are being watched."

Jack began to pace. "Look, I have a feeling that these people who are after us already know where we are. Think about it. With satellites and tracking gear, they can find anyone, anywhere. Paris and I drove in from the airport. How many cameras do you think we passed during that time? Hundreds! They know where we are, I'll bet you. It wouldn't surprise me if they wanted us to find Monroe so they could rig it where nobody else ever could. I say we go out in the open and do this thing. We'll find Blanch's house if it's still there and find Monroe. We start with the Reservoir and look for Hope's marker. It'll be hard, sure, but for some reason we have all been pulled into this. I want us all out." Jack walked over to Maggie, sat down beside her and said, "All of us."

"You're asking for trouble here, Jack. You know that," Paris said.

"We got trouble already, darlin'," Jack replied.

"You got that right!" Wood said. "Has anybody seen my lighter?"

"What happens if all this plays out?" Lovey began. "What happens if we by chance find Monroe in some wall somewhere? What then? What happens then? Do we call the Historical Society? Do we hold a press conference? Get a forensic team in there to do some science on the body to determine the fifth President is not who everyone grew up to think he was? I'm at a loss here. You say you want this over, Jack. Well how does finding a walled-up corpse end anything?"

"I don't know!" Jack yelled. "I don't know. I found that ledger for a reason. I truly believe that. I have to see this through, and I think that walled up corpse is the key."

"We have to play it out, Jack," Maggie said. "I was with you when you found it, remember?"

"I was the one who hauled the trunk around all those years," Wood mumbled.

"I was the one who knew it was evil and opened the door anyway," Lovey said, still feeling guilty.

Then everyone looked at Paris who was standing there still taking it all in.

"You aren't a part of this," Maggie remarked. "You need to go. You don't need to be with us in this, it could get dangerous. All you did was try to help Jack. You saw me as a dangerous woman and you tried to protect your friend. I see that. You need to go away from here. This isn't your fight. It's ours."

"I led a friend of mine into a bad situation over this," Paris reminded them. "I didn't know it would get him arrested. All he wanted to do was to take me to dinner. I led him on, and now he's in jail or maybe not even alive. I did that. Not you. That makes me an accessory in all this. I'm staying for a guy who never asked for any of this and for my boss who took a bullet. I don't even know if it's related, but to tell you the truth, I just don't have any place else to go. So, if you don't mind, I'm staying in it. Besides, it might make a good book some day."

"Alright then. It's settled," Jack declared. "We go to Virginia in the morning and finish this. We don't come back until we know one way or another if Monroe is there."

A knock at the door jarred them from their conversation. As the door opened everyone braced for the worse, then, "Supper time!" It was Grace with a huge basket of food. Everyone let out a sigh of relief.

"You old bitch. You scared the shit outta us!" Wood barked as he got up to help Grace in with the food. "I forgive you this time. I'm starving!"

"So where are we with all the intrigue tonight? You figure out why people want you dead?" Grace asked as she started setting up the table.

"Yeah, it's a mess Grace. We got to go to Virginia tomorrow. Fix things, you know?" Wood said while going for the food.

Grace glanced around the room and said, "Virginia tomorrow? Pete needs the cabin this weekend. That'll work out."

Paris sat silent as Grace chatted and finally said, "Hello, I'm Paris."

Jack explained, "Grace, Paris is a friend of mine from work. She's helping us get through this."

Grace glanced at Maggie. "How's your head, darlin'? You look like shit. You sure you want to travel? Air pressure in a plane can cause headaches and you got one goin' in. I'd watch that."

"I'm fine," she confided. "I sure wish I knew who hit me. I can't remember any of it. I went to bed and woke up in Lovey's room with a headache."

"I sure remember it," Lovey said. "It was crazy! You ran in and almost killed me. Somebody took an old envelope I had. It's really strange. I can't figure out who would want it. It's the missing piece of the puzzle."

"Someone took what? An envelope?" Paris asked. "Jesus! Where do you people find all this shit? What was in that one, or dare I ask?"

"It was summons and death certificate records from 1801. I found where Daniel Blanch's wife, Hope, was hung as a witch. I was sitting on the bed with it and then Maggie ran in and attacked me. It was really Blanch, I think. I was passing out and saw someone, but I couldn't make out whom. They took the envelope."

"See? I told you Hope was hung as a witch," Jack said to Paris, who just shook her head in disbelief.

"Who could have taken it?" Paris asked.

"Who could have burned down my Barn?" Maggie asked. "Who took the envelope Lovey said she found? Why am I channeling Daniel Blanch? Why are we here in a cabin hiding out like convicts? We didn't ask for any of this, yet here we are. Tomorrow we are going to Virginia to look for…. It's all too much. I'm exhausted. I'm going back to bed," Maggie said as she let go of some emotions.

Wood sat there looking at everyone and said, "Man, this is some real Hardy Boys shit here!"

Chapter 25

THE 599

Later that evening, The Snowman sat at his computer and looked at the flash drive given to him by agent Bill Cantrell. He looked up at the Miami Vice poster with a reverence and shook his head. "How do you guys pull it all off?" he said aloud. Then, positioning himself, he took a deep breath, inserted the flash drive and accessed the files. As he studied the databases Cantrell had given him to hack, he wondered what could be so important? One by one he approached the firewalls. As he was granted access, he let out a sigh of relief for each one. In a half an hour he was done. The files were repositioned on the flash drive and he sat back, cracked his knuckles and waited for what was to come. It was 10:32PM.

After a successful hack it was customary to play a war game to "cleanse his soul." As he picked up his trusty controller, he wondered if this would be the last time he ever played anything. The game began and he sat and waited. Hours passed. He stopped the game and sat and listened for the sound of anything. It was all too quiet.

At 6:45am he awoke, still in his chair. He rose up, looked around the room and found nothing out of the ordinary. Did he just make it through the night? He stood up, stretched his back and glanced down at his computer. The flash drive was gone. He looked around on the floor, on the desk, everywhere. It was nowhere to be found. Getting up, he headed for his kitchen. As he passed his front window he happened to glance out in the driveway and saw a silver Ferrari 599 sitting there.

"The car!" He fumbled with the doorknob, then ran out into the driveway like it was a hundred Christmas mornings all rolled into one. The Ferrari 599 was his dream car. Now, there was one in his driveway. He walked around it and inspected every panel. When he got to the back of the car, a prestige tag read "SNOWMAN." He stared at it a second and then said, "So much for hacker anonymity. Agent Baker, you son of a bitch." He opened the door, got in and looked around. "Incredible!" he exclaimed. He then explored the dash and hit the button for the glove compartment. When he did, it opened and a Glock pistol was revealed. That's when one word came blazing into his mind. "Paris!"

Steven landed hard from his little journey into fantasyland. As great as the car was, the price was going to be staggeringly high. He took out the gun and held it in his hand. The car, the gun, the contract, the payday and six months on the island all were floating through his head. Then, "Paris. How in the world am I gonna kill Paris?"

Taking a deep sigh, he put the gun back in the glove box. The blue tooth key chain lay on the console and he wondered how he was going to get out of this. For now, he was hungry and the McDonald's drive through had just opened. He started up the car and it purred like the fancy cat it was. He took the long way around getting there. Along the way he waved at every living soul he passed.

Steven turned on the GPS where a destination was already entered. "Fredericksburg, Virginia," he said aloud after he read it, "Now how did I know that?"

After his McDonald's run he sat down at his computer and assumed he was being shadowed. His screen was probably showing up somewhere on somebody else's screen. That's where the fun began. He never mentioned to Agent Baker that while he was in the system making him look like Dorothy in a dress, he happened to build himself a back door into their system. He needed only to go in, find everything they had on him and wipe it out. That, however, was too easy. Another idea came to mind.

By noon he was well on his way to Virginia. The Ferrari was everything he dreamed of. Wearing his coveted Sonny Crocket signature Miami Vice white satin shirt, halfway unbuttoned of course, and dated aviator sunglasses he was cruisin' large. In his mind all he could think of was Paris. He knew there was no way in hell he could kill anybody. Fate had landed him in the driver's seat of what could well be his last few hours on the planet. At least if he had to go out, he was going to do it in style.

It was a nine-hour drive to Fredericksburg. He wondered why Paris would be in Fredericksburg, but regardless, that's where he was going. And quite fast at that.

Chapter 26

RESERVOIR TIME

Jack, Maggie, Wood, Lovey and Paris arrived in Virginia at the Ronald Reagan Airport near Washington, D.C. It was an hour drive to Fredericksburg, so they opted to rent a large S.U.V. for comfort. As they pulled into Fredericksburg, Maggie seemed agitated.

"This is where Abigail Long died," Maggie remembered. As they passed the Bowden facility, she looked up at the stone walls and said, "Yep. Bye-bye Abigail."

Jack felt like he was driving a band of outlaws headed for a job. He shook his head and wondered how he had ended up here in Virginia. They were in search of a two-hundred-year-old unmarked grave that if found, would let them know that the possible remains of James Monroe lay nearby. Blanch had buried his wife near their little house beside a 'waterfault'. In that house, behind a wall, was evidence of a cover up that would change history.

Paris took out the pamphlet that Jack and Wood were given at the Fredericksburg Courthouse that showed the location of the reservoir. She served as navigator for Jack and led them to the parking area. As they pulled in, Maggie declared immediately, "She's here."

"Who's here?" Jack asked.

"Hope Blanch is here. I know it!" Maggie said, getting out of the car. "I've been here before. It's different, but I've been here before."

Maggie began walking down a path by the reservoir, which was about ten acres of water by a hillside. "It's down here." Maggie motioned for them to follow her.

They came to a bend in the trail and then she stopped, turned and walked off the trail up the hill into the woods. It was getting thick and wooded when she stopped and turned to face the water. "It's here. Here is where Hope sat."

Jack turned and looked at the landscape. He was facing the smooth water of the reservoir and there was a hill behind it that would have "made the sun set first" like Blanch had said in the ledger. "This looks right," Jack observed. "Maggie, can you remember where Blanch put her marker? Where is the stone?"

Maggie looked around at the ground. "It's here."

Jack looked at Wood and said, "Dig!"

They began to clear out the area as best they could, moving weeds, logs, old limbs, everything moveable, leaving only the bare ground.

Wood seemed frustrated. "Now what? We got nothin'."

"Wait," Maggie said. She closed her eyes and began to go into a trance. Lovey stepped up and warned, "Careful Mags. Don't let him out."

Maggie knelt down to the soft ground and let her hand move slowly in circles in the soft dark topsoil. As she got deeper into the ground, she felt something. She kept moving her hand around until she had uncovered a two-foot square stone. She tried to pull it up but couldn't. The four watched in amazement. At last Jack knelt down beside her. "Let me help you."

As Maggie stood up, Jack dug his fingers into the ground around the stone and pulled up. The buried rock turned over and Jack began to clear away the mud that lay on it. Letters came into view. One by one H-O-P-E was revealed. They just stared at it.

"Well, what now?" Jack asked, looking up from the stone. "We found Hope's marker. Now what? I guess the house is somewhere near here."

Maggie turned around and instinctively faced the hill behind her. "It's up there."

The five of them left Hope's stone facedown, the way they found it, and headed up the wooded hillside. When they reached the top, they were met with a chain link fence. Through the fence was a sea of tombstones and a sign that read, "Fredericksburg Cemetery. Keep Out."

"It's a graveyard!" Lovey exclaimed as they stood there looking over it. "Now what?"

Maggie kept looking over the property. "It's over there. That house there, with the lawn mowers. That's it!"

Jack was confused. "Maggie, that's a tool shed. That's no house."

Maggie was confident. "That's it! That's where Blanch lived. I can tell. Trust me. That's it!"

"How do we get over there?" Paris asked as she studied the fence. "I'm no fence climber."

Jack surveyed the area and said, "It's a public cemetery. Let's just go through the front gate. It's not like it's guarded or anything. We aren't doing anything wrong. We are simply tourists looking for an old relative or something." The five of them followed the fence around to the gate and walked in. "Look reverent," Jack whispered as they passed people already milling around the area.

"How does that look?" Wood whispered back.

"Just walk naturally," Lovey whispered as they passed the concrete monuments.

"Why are you guys whispering?" Jack asked.

"I hate these places," Paris proclaimed. "I never go to funerals."

Maggie walked trancelike through the paths of the cemetery. "It's over here."

At last they had come to the tool shed. They looked around and saw no one near, so they opened the wooden door and went inside.

Jack looked around. "This is no mortar house, it's a barn. Maggie, are you sure about this?"

Maggie once more closed her eyes. Then, slowly looked down at the ground. "It's down there. It's under us. This shed was built on top of the house. The body is under us!"

"But how do we get down there?" Paris asked, as she kicked the hard floor.

"I guess you start digging," came a voice from the door.

They all turned around to see Grace, Sam Hecker and Sue, the insurance inspector, standing in the doorway with Sam holding a gun pointed right at them.

Paris turned to Jack. "What the hell? Jack, what's goin' on?"

Jack stood there staring at the three people he had trusted standing in the doorway. "You've got to be kidding me! You're involved in this? How? What are you doing here?"

Maggie stood silent as Lovey spoke to her brother, "Sam, please."

"It's got to be, Audrey. I told you it was time. Everything is coming together. It's unavoidable. It's all coming true," Sam said in a smooth and easy tone.

"Will somebody clue me in on what's going on?" Paris insisted.

Grace stood contentedly and explained, "You're standing in the middle of a transition, Paris. A transition of power that's been coming together for over two hundred years."

Jack kept staring at Sam's gun and asked, "What transition of power? This is bullshit!"

"No, it's not," Grace continued. "We always knew someone would lead us to her, but we never knew when. A lot of people tried, but never quite made it here until you, Jack Reynolds. You walked right in, took the bait and here we are."

"Bait?" Jack barked. "What bait?"

"Do you know how many people we sent over to Maggie's from the bar?" Grace laughed. "Did you really think our little Wall of Shame was simply a poster board for drunks? Everyone on there is dead now because they failed to do what you did."

"Dead?" Jack questioned. "Dead how?"

Grace walked up and stood in front of Jack as if to stare him down. "Given to the spirit of Hope Blanch. Sam found people all up and down that road you were on. You think it's a coincidence your tire blew when it did and Sam just happened to be coming up that road behind you? He'd been following you since you last got gas down the mountain. He shot your tire out from under you!"

"I thought getting a cop when I needed one was a reach," Jack said coldly, as he felt himself getting more and more angry.

"Think about it. He picks you up, takes you to a bar that just happened to have a wrecker sitting beside it and then a place for you to stay the night? That's quite a jump there, partner. Didn't you think it was a little odd that nobody paid attention to you coming out of that little closet the next morning? Do the math, Jack. You were set up from the pickup!"

"No way! What about evidence? The other people had cars, things to show they were at the Grizzly Beer. What happened to all that?"

"Tony down where you and Maggie picked up your car? Him? He runs a chop shop that took all the cars away. It was quite a shock to him when somebody actually showed up to pick up a car. Nobody ever had before."

"And what did I do that nobody else did, besides be a sucker?" Jack said coldly.

"Simply fall in love with her," Grace replied. "We knew anyone who fell for her would follow her anywhere to find the Monroe legend. All this was never about finding the body of James Monroe. It was always about finding the gravesite of the Queen Mother of all our magic. The first one." Grace pointed to Maggie and exclaimed, "Hope Blanch is alive in us all! Especially in her!"

Maggie stepped backwards and said, "No! I don't know anything about Hope. She was Daniel Blanch's wife. Lovey says I have been channeling him to get us here."

"I'm afraid you were never channeling Daniel Blanch, my dear." Grace began. "You've been channeling Hope. When Lovey took you into the past life regression, it revived her in you. She is why you had yourself locked up at that nuthouse for fourteen months in the first place. You were trying to get her out of your head. She chose you. It's an honor. But you denied her!"

"But I felt it! Daniel Blanch was in love with Elizabeth Kortright. I saw it in a regression. It was real!" Maggie retorted, obviously shaken.

"You felt Hope, not Daniel!" Grace snapped. "Hope was in love with Elizabeth. She was trying to get Elizabeth to come back and live with her, but Spence Monroe got in the way."

"Then you know about James Monroe, the twin, all the deceit?" Maggie asked cautiously.

"You really don't know, do you?" Grace replied as she walked towards her. "Where do you think the ledger came from? All that writing? The descriptions? It came from you! You wrote that ledger and put it in the trunk! You were in one of your Hope induced trances. We were there. We saw you sit with a quill and a well of ink, writing your tale of murder and deception. It was magical!

Sam and Sue nodded. "She's right, Maggie," Sue added. "We were there. We saw you."

Maggie looked at Sue and said, "I can't believe you're a part of this. Where's your partner? He in on this, too?"

"Williams?" Sue laughed. "Hell no! He hasn't a clue. I had to act like I wanted to have sex with you so he wouldn't catch on that I already had been with you, many times. But it wasn't you. It was Hope. Hope wanted me, through you!"

"This is insane!" Maggie started. "I had sex with you? Many times? I wrote the ledger? I drew the tools? I don't believe it. Any of it!"

"You didn't draw the tools, Maggie," Sam said. "When we found Daniel Blanch's ledger, the tools were already there. He drew them. He was a genius. He came up with ideas far beyond his time. When you saw, or Hope saw, the drawings she was pulled to it. She, or you, simply wrote the Monroe legend in the back of the ledger Daniel had drawn his tools in. After all, you, or Hope, were really married to Blanch and had a daughter, Pamela. Daniel Blanch was your distant grandfather."

"What?' Maggie snapped. "Me? I didn't write anything in the ledger. I'd never seen it before Jack and I found it in the trunk!"

"And how do you think you and Jack found it in the first place?" Grace asked. "It was the saw! You told us while you were channeling Hope that a man would come to lead the way "who was in search of tools." When Jack asked me in the bar if you had any old tools in the Barn, I knew the prophecy was coming true. I knew it was Jack! When he saw the old saw under the trunk, it was the starting point to a new era for us. The tools Blanch had drawn in the front of the ledger were always meant for Jack to find. Hope saw it. Through you!"

"I don't believe it!" Jack said. "I took that ledger because I was looking for a birthday present for my boss back in Georgia. It was originally for him. I told you that."

"Yes, you did." Grace admitted. "That's why Sam here went down there and put a bullet through Seth Holiday's head. So you would keep the ledger!"

"What?" Both Jack and Paris said at the same time. "You killed Seth over the ledger? He didn't know anything about the damn thing!" Jack yelled.

"Not then he didn't," Grace continued. "We couldn't risk Seth Holiday having it, so we took him out."

"I don't believe it!" Paris argued. "I was followed by someone that morning in a black Lincoln. I think they did it."

Sam stepped towards Paris. "You want to hear it? I flew down and called Holiday on Friday night just before he went home. I told him I wanted to buy ten cabins for my campground, and would he meet me the next morning. So, on Saturday morning I parked my rented Lincoln on an overlook up the mountain, hiked down, met Holiday and he showed me around the place. I made up a story about how I'd already given my finance info to Jack. We go in Jack's office to look for the info and I did him there. Jack's office was in the middle of the building. Guns make noise. His office was the safest part of the building where nobody outside would hear the shot.

I hiked back up, got in the car, and pulled out. I didn't know it was you in the car I was pulling out behind. When I saw you pull into Holiday Cabins, I went down the street and waited to see if you found the body. By the way all those cop cars swarmed in, I assumed you did, so I left. And here we are."

"That was you in the Lincoln!" Paris snapped at Sam. "You killed my friend? Over a goddamn book he didn't even have! Damn you!"

"We couldn't risk Jack finding it and then just giving it away to some guy to put in his tool collection," Sue said. "Jack and Maggie had to keep the ledger. It was always meant for them to find together. Sorry about your friend."

Jack looked at Sam with an anger he'd never known. He was furious.

Grace continued explaining to Maggie, "Your writing in the ledger looked so authentic we knew it had to be Hope coming through you. It was at the mountain, Maggie, seven years ago. And then you had it all erased. Your whole life as Abigail Long was just wiped out. You were hypnotized in that hospital to forget it. Brainwashed! Hope WAS here Maggie! You are the channel to her. It's always been you."

Jack, now blindsided by Grace's recollections said, "You mean Maggie wrote the ledger? No way! It's in old script! Pen and ink? Maggie, do you remember writing the ledger?"

"No! I didn't write it. I couldn't have. It's old and on ancient parchment paper. There's no way."

"I thought the ink looked different," Paris said. "When I first saw the ledger there was a discrepancy in the tone of the ink, like it was written at another time."

"Oh, she is good, Jack. You got yourself a winner here!" Grace said mockingly.

"Why me? I don't understand? Why would I be chosen?" Maggie wondered aloud, as she searched herself for answers.

"So you could lead us to Hope," Grace replied. "It's written that the one who is led to her will be the next High Priest. That someone was you, Maggie, until the fire at your place stopped you from going to Virginia. Then it turned into Jack going with Wood. I've got to say, we never expected that, but here we are."

"Led who to what? Make sense woman! All this is crazy!" Jack said.

"The High Priest of our clan will be led to her willingly by an outsider," Grace said. "And you did that Jack. You led him here."

"I led who here?" Jack said.

"Me, Jack," Wood said, stepping over to Grace. "You led me here. I am the next High Priest."

Lovey was standing in shock. "Wood! What are you doing? We left to get away from all this! We told ourselves it was done!"

"Sorry, doll. Just couldn't let it go," Wood confessed.

"All this time you've been in touch with them. The birds. You've been using the pigeons all this time." Lovey put the pieces together and looked at Wood in disappointment.

"They are handy little things," Grace said. "Real handy despite the pigeon shit on my truck!"

"Oh, Dad," Maggie said. "This isn't you. Tell me this isn't you."

"She's coming to us through you, Maggie," Sue said. "She's been living through you until now. Soon she will live on through Wood, our new High Priest."

"High Priest? Wood? What a fucking joke! Wait. If you thought I was the chosen one to lead Wood here, then you had to have been here when we were here last, in case we found Hope's grave," Jack concluded.

"Yeah. That's right, Jack," Wood admitted. "Remember when I told you to look around and I'd stay by the waterfall? Sam, Grace, Sue and I scoured that damned place and we didn't find a thing. We went back there that night. The night you thought I was at the porno movie? I was with them at the falls looking for a rock with 'Hope' written on it. As you can see, we never found it."

"I don't believe it," Maggie said. "It's all a blur. I could never have been a part of something like this. So the goal is to find Hope's grave?"

"Her grave, body and amulet. She is wearing an amulet that's very old. Whoever has that amulet will rule as High Priest," Grace confirmed.

"Oh, come on people! What century are you living in?" Jack started. "High Priests? Witches and amulets? You people are insane!"

"So tell me," Maggie demanded, "Who did it? Who burned my Barn down? Was it you Grace? You playing head games with me to get me to come here?"

"I gotta say," Grace insisted, "I didn't have a thing to do with it. That place went up like a torch at three in the morning. We called the fire department and that's all we know."

"I don't believe you," Maggie said accusingly.

"Believe her, Maggie, Lovey said. "Grace didn't set your barn on fire. I did. Me and Pete."

Maggie turned to Lovey with a shocked look. "You! Lovey, why? How did you do it? You were with us!"

"I called Pete that night and I told him what you had found. I said it was evil and that we needed to get rid of it. After that coven shit that tore our family apart, I knew Pete would do it. He knows how powerful that damned ledger is. When I told him there was more stuff in the Barn, he agreed that it was too dangerous to let you find it. Pete torched it. He left the red gas cans out behind the place like an idiot!"

"But Pete is one of us," Grace said. "He wouldn't do that!"

Lovey began to pace. "He wanted out like I did. You remember what hell he gave me for leaving? We've barely spoken for years!"

"Why?" Maggie pleaded. "Why'd you have him burn down the Barn?"

Jack stepped up and said, "Because she didn't realize the ledger and trunk were in the outbuilding behind it. She couldn't risk us finding anything else related to the ledger so she had Pete torch the place, thinking it would wipe out all traces of anything to do with the ledger."

Lovey nodded. "That's right, Jack. You are good. I couldn't risk it. I knew it was evil and I wanted to destroy it. Then we found the notebook inside the ledger. I believed the Monroe tale actually could be true. I'm sorry about the Barn, Maggie. I know you loved that place."

"You had Pete burn it down!" Wood said, disgusted. "All for nothing, it seems. Oh, Lovey I wish you had talked to me first."

"Where did the notebook come from?" Jack demanded. "If you say Maggie wrote the ledger, what about the notebook in the binding of the ledger and that pamphlet we found in the trunk? Where did those come from? They're not a forgery too, are they?"

"No. Maggie found the pamphlet when she was doing her research on James Monroe for her master's degree," Grace said. "It was in a library somewhere, unmarked. She recognized it for what it was and stole it. We sewed it in the back of the ledger."

"That's a lie!" Maggie snapped. "I'd never seen that notebook until I took it out of the back of that ledger!"

"Sorry darlin'. But you did. You did it all. Now here we are!" Sue exclaimed.

"So you expect me to believe that I just turn into Hope Blanch and write ledgers and such so Wood can be a High Priest of a witch coven?" Maggie asked, now highly agitated.

"Pretty much. Now we are going to prove it to you," Sam

said. "You told us you'd been here before. You talked to us as Hope and told us you had given gifts to her. Now we'll find out."

Sam began looking down at the ground and moving things. "There has to be a way down there," he insisted. "You said you were here, Maggie. Where is the door? Think! Look for it."

Maggie looked around the room and closed her eyes. Images flickered on and off in her mind as she tried to remember a time when she was in the cemetery tool barn. Then her eyes focused on a closet. "There!" she said, "It's in there. How do I know that?"

Sam went to the door, opened it and pulled out rakes, shovels and other old tools then cleared away the floor. "There's a lever!" he called out as he pulled up on it. When he did, he uncovered a dark hole in the floor. "This must be it!"

The others gathered around and Sam took a flashlight down off the wall nearby. He shined the light down the hole and found steps to a ladder leading down to the bottom. Picking up a shovel he said, "In you go!" Sam pointed to Lovey, Maggie, Jack and Paris. "Come on. Get in the hole!"

Jack took the first move. "Hand me the light," he said. "Look, it's fucking dark down there. I need a light!"

Sam handed him the flashlight and Jack descended. Maggie, Paris, and Lovey followed, then the rest. At the bottom was a dirt floor and musty, moldy walls. Jack shone the light around and saw large bags stacked up on the far wall of the space they were in.

"What's that?" Paris asked.

"Check it out," Grace ordered Jack as she pointed the gun at him.

Jack walked over to the four bags and untied one. When he pulled back the plastic a body was revealed.

"Shit!" Jack said, as he jumped back. "Looks like we're not alone down here."

Maggie walked over to the bodies and said to Jack, "Give me the light."

She shined the light on the face of the corpse and took a startled breath as she fell backwards into Paris.

"What the hell is it? You know that face?" Jack asked.

"He was my student. I knew him. He was one of the ones…." And she stopped.

Paris glanced down at the body and said, "He was one of the ones you were charged with killing, but got off because no bodies were ever found. The other three bags are probably the remaining three. It appears you did kill those students and you brought them here. Remember, Maggie? You were found innocent. Then you went to the Bowden hospital for fourteen months until you got your shit straight enough to move to Colorado. You bought the Antique Barn, changed your name to Maggie Styles from Abigail Long and started over."

"Paris does it again! Oh, she is good!" Grace said. "Jack, I see why you wanted her around. These are the gifts you brought to Hope, Maggie. You said you brought her something. I had no idea it was souls. She must have been pleased!"

Maggie stood there in astonishment. "It was true! It was all true! I am a killer! I murdered those four students from school and brought them here, put them in this place and then returned unaware of any of it. I swore I had nothing to do with it. It was the lie detector tests that cleared me. I really had no knowledge of it. Oh my God, I did it! I did it all! Everything they said!" Maggie began to shake, feeling weak and nauseous.

"Not you, Maggie. Hope!" Wood clarified her revelation. He gave Grace an approving look. "Now let's see her. Jack, take this shovel and put a hole in that corner wall. That's where she ought to be. Hope will have the amulet and that'll be it."

"I thought Hope was outside near the water," Paris questioned.

"No. She's here," Wood insisted.

"I thought James Monroe was here," Lovey stated.

"There never was a James Monroe you idiot!" Grace yelled at Lovey. "It's always been about this moment. Nobody would want to find a two hundred year old woman who was hung as a witch. There were hundreds of them. But when Maggie found the Monroe notebook doing her research, she saw the angle. Hope must have led her to it. You've been on a wild goose chase, but you just caught a different goose. Now dig! Let's see her!"

Jack took the shovel, went to the wall and began to stab it. The soft mortar fell away as a hollow space was revealed beneath. As Jack pulled out a large stone, burlap wrapping was revealed.

"It's her!" Wood exclaimed. "The Queen herself!"

Jack continued moving away the rock and then the burlap wrapping fell forward. They all froze. Maggie began to shake and could feel Hope stirring inside her. Standing in front of the body she sensed a connection she couldn't explain.

Grace knelt down and removed the wrapping and stared into the two hundred year old face of Hope Blanch and gasped. Wood came over and pulled down the cloth, revealing a chain around the fragile bones. He lifted it from her neck and a golden carved amulet with a large yellow stone came into view.

Maggie glared at the amulet and felt Hope's dark life force leave her and occupy the stone that sparkled in the flashlight's beam. Sam, Sue, and Grace anxiously watched Wood slide the amulet chain from Hope's neck. He was about to put it around his own when he turned to Grace and said, "We've waited a long time for this."

Grace laid the gun down next to her, closed her eyes and bowed down on one knee. Sam and Sue got down and bowed their heads as well, Wood leaned down, picked up the gun and said, "Fuck it! I never believed any of this shit anyway!" He then hit Sam on the side of the head with the gun and Sam fell back unconscious. Wood pointed the gun at Grace and Sue and said, "Get over there by the bags!"

"Wood! What are you doing? We are here. It's your turn! The amulet! Take it and claim your place as High Priest." Sue cried out as she watched in total shock.

"Do I look like a High Priest?" Wood yelled. "Please! I went along with this shit you came up with for Maggie. I wanted her to have some sense of who she really was and show her she is a witch in good time. She's a direct descendant of Hope and Daniel Blanch.

Maggie and Jack said, "What?"

Wood looked at Maggie. "You know it. You're a witch, kiddo. So am I, so are Grace and Lovey. Descendants of a magic over two hundred years old.

I was tired of living with the killing of all those people whose picture Grace displayed on that stupid Wall of Shame.

Wood turned to Grace and said, "You wouldn't leave us alone. You kept at me. Finally, I figured we'd see how it played. Everything was just Fantasy Island until a few days ago when Maggie showed up in Florida with Jack and that damned ledger. I saw her happy for once. The old spark was back in her eyes again. I never thought any of this would happen."

Wood held the gun out and took the flashlight.

"I knew that summons envelope was in the trunk. I had it hidden away for good until Lovey went and found the thing. She brought it home and Pete had to get it back."

Wood turned to Lovey and said, "Pete watched you take that envelope, Lovey. He knew what it was. He helped me put it in there. He didn't count on Maggie going ape shit on you, though. That's when he ran in and hit Maggie and took it. Lucky for you he happened to be there. He had to get it away from Lovey before she figured out it was Hope in the wall and not James Monroe. It was all in there. That's how we knew all of this. That's why it was hidden in the bottom of the trunk."

"I have a question," Paris began. "If this is Hope, who walled her up here? Blanch didn't, so who did?"

Maggie looked up and calmly said, "She did. I understand

it all now. Hope wanted to make sure she was buried with the amulet so one day someone could retrieve it. There could be no risk of anyone stealing it. She wrapped herself in burlap when she knew death was near, put the amulet around her neck, then walled herself up in this place and died."

"But her death certificate said she was hung as a witch," Lovey said. "I read it!"

Maggie continued. "Hope was powerful. She was hung as the witch she was, rose up off the pile of the dead and walked away unnoticed. She lived out her life in seclusion until Daniel Blanch died, then she walled herself up in here. A forgotten woman preserving herself for two hundred years, entombed here. She wrote, through me, that it was Monroe in the wall to ensure somebody would keep searching until she was found."

"All this was planned?" Jack retorted. "I was played from the start." He then turned to Maggie and said, "Played like the fool I am about everything that's happened this last week."

"Not everything," Maggie said looking into his face. "There was no denying that we had a connection. You felt it just like I did. We still do have that Jack. That is, if you want us to have it. What I feel for you has nothing to do with Hope and the amulet. Please believe that."

"This is all real sweet, but we got something that needs doing here," Wood reminded them. He then looked at Jack and handed him the gun. Jack took it and stared at Sue and Grace in front of him still down on their knees. Wood took the amulet and held it up in the air and watched it spin around and glow in the dark. He laid it down on the big rock Jack had pulled out of the wall and picked up a smaller rock.

"It's got to end here, Grace. No more High Priests. No more killing innocent people for Hope. It stops here. After two hundred years it stops here."

Wood took the rock and raised it back over his shoulder. Grace looked at him and yelled out, "Nooooo!" Wood let the rock strike the amulet, shattering its stone to tiny pieces on the cold damp dirt floor. As it shattered, Maggie grabbed her chest and fell to the floor unconscious.

Jack leaned down to her and felt her neck. "She's alive!" he said. "But she's out cold."

Grace and Sue felt the pain as well. Sam woke up from being hit on the head and clenched his chest like Sue and Grace. Grace slowly got up and looked at the others and cried out, "She's gone. My God, Hope's gone! I don't feel her anymore. I've felt Hope for so long I didn't know anything else."

Sam stood up and looked around the room at the bodies on the floor. "What did we do, Grace? Look at what we did."

"It was Hope, not you, Grace," Wood said, recovering from his own shock. "This is why Lovey and I left for Florida. She was a part of us too, until we got away. Hope left us a little at a time, but you must be feeling a kick! It had to be done. I had to find the amulet to destroy it. I couldn't let you continue in all that killing in her name."

Maggie began to stir in Jack's arms. A low moan and then her eyes opened.

"Hey! Nutty professor. You Okay?" Jack teased as Maggie came around.

As Maggie rose up, she looked around the room and remembered where she was. "I'm ....ok...I think." Jack helped her up.

"Mags, what happened to you?" Lovey asked gently.

"It's over. I don't feel her anymore. I've never felt this free," Maggie mused, looking around the room.

"Hope has been in you your whole life, Maggie," Wood told her. "Blanch was really your great-great grandfather, that much is real. Hope lived down our family tree. She was a powerful witch in her day, and you have that magic still inside you. It's something you can't shake, so get used to it getting stronger as time passes. And it's time we got out of this hole!"

"Amen to that!" Sam agreed. "What about the bodies? Do we leave them here?"

"Well, they've been here for a while and nobody's found them yet." I say we just back out of here," Sue suggested.

"I feel sorry for them," Maggie said as she pointed to the bags on the ground. "They trusted me. I'll never know how they got here or how I killed them."

"You didn't. Hope did. Remember that," Lovey reminded her as she put her arm around Maggie.

As they climbed up out of the hole and back into the tool shed, Sam covered everything up the way he found it. "Nobody will ever know. Let's….hope!"

As they were walking down the cemetery sidewalk, Paris heard the sound of the Miami Vice soundtrack coming from in front of her. She looked up and saw Steven, The Snowman, leaning up against the silver Ferrari 599, his shirt halfway unbuttoned and wearing dark shades. "I don't believe it!" She exclaimed in surprise.

"You know that guy?" Jack asked as they approached him.

"It's the Snowman, Jack!" Paris said as she walked over to him.

"You need a ride home?" Steven said, as coolly as possible.

"I don't ride in fast cars with anonymous people," she joked. Paris then smiled, put her arms around him and said, "I'm not going to ask why or how you are here."

Steven looked at her and said, "I was contracted by shady people in some black ops outfit to kill you, because they thought you and Jack together could actually prove something dangerous to someone high up the chain. And believe it or not, I don't want to know any more about it!"

"Kill me?" Paris said.

"They thought as long as you and Jack were working together, you could pretty much get into any system you wanted because you knew me. They knew I could dodge them, so the only sure bet was for me to take you out of the equation. They'd have your murder pinned on me as leverage for me to work for them when they needed me to."

"So now I've got to worry about some shady agency chasing me?" Paris asked.

"Relax. It's all good." Steven reassured her. "They let me in their system to do some clever Photoshop work on one of their agents named Baker. I made myself a back door while I was in and now, they are busy trying to figure out how to break the ping-pong firewall I built for their computer framework. They'll be chasing it until it stops in 2025."

"Must suck to be them," Paris smirked. "So, The Snowman strikes again!"

"Let's just say I'm keeping the guys who wanted you permanently out of the way busy with another agenda. By the way, have you ever been to Miami?"

Paris waved to Jack and the rest as she and Steven got in the Ferrari and sped down the road. "I'll call you!" Paris yelled over the roar of the car.

Maggie turned to Jack, "So, Jack Reynolds, prefabricated cabin salesman from Georgia, you got somebody waiting to take you away, too?"

"Oh, I don't know. I might be moving up to the mountains. I hear it's gorgeous up there," Jack teased as he kissed her.

Chapter 27

BIG MEDICINE

When the plane landed in Colorado, everyone got off and felt the ground of home. As they were walking back to their cars, Grace turned to Wood. "It's done, Wood. It's over. Hope had reached us all from the grave. Until that amulet was smashed, I would have killed for her. Now I feel like an old foolish woman."

"That's because you are an old foolish woman!" Wood laughed out loud. "So, we good?"

"Yeah, I guess. Say, why don't you and Lovey move back up? Now that the coven is gone, seems weird you're staying in Florida."

"Nah, it isn't the same. The Barn's gone; I got my birds who like it down there and I don't miss the snow one bit." Wood responded with conviction as he looked at Lovey. "Besides, me and Lovey got a great hook up for some good weed!"

Sam looked up. "Look who's here," as Pete came walking towards them. "Hey brother!" Sam said.

Pete looked at Grace and Sam. "I know it's over. We all felt it up here. It's like the sky cleared in our minds. What happened? Did you find Hope? You must have!"

Grace said, "Let's just say she's gone. The amulet was destroyed so it will never control anyone again. Let's go home."

Sam and Pete walked over to Lovey and asked, "Audrey, come back home. Let's go back to the way things were when we were kids." Then, for the first time in years, the three hugged and felt the strength of family again.

"Call me Lovey! 'Audrey' just feels weird." She laughed as she hugged both her brothers.

"That's some big medicine there!" Wood laughed as they walked towards the car.

"Been a long time coming," Grace said. "This whole chain of events has been a long time coming."

The crowd at Christie's auction house was filled to capacity. The next item on the block was a personal notebook owned by James Monroe, the fifth President of the United States and a pamphlet written by him entitled "A View of the Conduct of the Executive in the Foreign Affairs of the United States."

The announcer stepped to the microphone and announced, "The bidding will start at one million dollars for the pair."

"A million clams!" Wood practically shouted. "Holy moly!"

"SHHHH!" Maggie whispered.

As the bidding began, the first bidding card rose, the auctioneer went higher, then higher and finally, "The bid stands at four and one half million dollars, do I hear four million seven? Going once, going twice, sold for four million five hundred thousand dollars!" The gavel sounded and the bidding war was over.

Jack, Maggie, Wood and Lovey sat there frozen.

"Did he just say that your books sold for over four million bucks?" Wood asked, sitting there in shock.

"I think he did," Jack replied happily as he looked at Maggie.

"They told me I have some papers to sign," Maggie told them. "I need to handle that. I'll meet you out front."

Maggie was ushered to the back offices of the building. She was taken into a room and the door closed behind her.

"Maggie Styles?" A little man said as he peered over the frame of his round wire glasses.

"Yes, I'm Maggie."

"Miss Styles," The man continued, "I'm Arthur Cloninger.

I'm the accountant for Christie's. Usually the buyers of historic articles for private collections want to remain anonymous, but in the case of the Monroe acquisitions, the buyer wants to meet you. Do you have a minute for him?"

Maggie looked around the room and replied, "Sure, I guess. Why does he want to meet me?"

"I'll let him tell you that." The little man got up and went to the door, opened it, and another man entered. "I'll be outside," Cloninger said as he left the room and closed the door.

Maggie stood silent as the man approached. "Maggie Styles, my name is Bill Cantrell. Have a seat."

She and Cantrell sat on a sofa in front of a large window.

"I have to say, we've been following this little notebook of yours with high interest ever since we learned of its existence," Cantrell began. "Admittedly, we didn't know what was in it, or its validity, but we knew it was something that had to be contained."

"Who's 'we'?" Maggie asked, being direct.

"Call us who you will, but the fact of the matter is we are simply people who wanted to take the Monroe notebook out of play. We stumbled on it by accident, really. Your friend Paris Frances was working with a Steven Winters. He goes by the name The Snowman when he's being an annoying little shit, hacking into places he shouldn't be."

"I just met him. Paris likes him," Maggie remembered. "I think he mentioned something about your firewall?"

"Yeah. We let him think he played hell with our system. He was never in our system. That wouldn't be smart on our part. It took some good acting by a couple of my men to let him think that, but really, to give someone like him access to our computer system would be foolish. Let's just say he was somewhere….else."

"So, you're saying he and Paris are still some kind of targets? Are they in danger?" Maggie asked.

"No. We like watching The Snowman and we may need him again for some specialty work, but have no plans to harm him or Paris Frances….now."

Cantrell sat back into the sofa and said," I guess you know

that the notebook is worth far more than what we paid? Am I right?"

"I was wondering if anyone but me knew that," Maggie sighed.

"If we hadn't tapped The Snowman's phone for hacking the Bowden facility and going after your old Abigail Long records, we'd have not known about the notebook at all. It was a fluke really. We tapped him, then Paris. On a hunch, we tapped Jack Reynolds. When you and Jack talked on the phone about the notebook our jaws hit the floor. The possibility of you actually finding James Monroe, the fifth President of the United States, walled up in some old building in Fredericksburg? His twin brother posing as him, fooling everyone? It's mind boggling! You can't make that up."

Maggie then knew that Cantrell only had half the story. It was the dark content of the ledger that kick started the whole thing. It was a ploy to get her and the others to find the amulet of Hope Blanch to usher in the new reign of a High Priest, not the body of James Monroe.

"So why didn't you guys just take us all out?" Maggie questioned. "Why let us keep going and then you pay for the notebook? I don't get it."

"It was the only way to be sure there was nothing more. If you had more personal artifacts of James Monroe, other than the notebook and his published pamphlet, you'd be trying to sell that as well. You're not, so we figure the situation is contained. Unless that is, I'm mistaken. Am I mistaken Maggie? Is this all there is to the Monroe situation?"

"No, Mister Cantrell. You're not mistaken. The situation is quite contained," Maggie assured him. "Let's.... hope."

Cantrell got up, opened the door, and the accountant returned. "Now we have papers to sign," he said.

Maggie met Jack, Wood, and Lovey at the front of the auction house. "Its all taken care of now. The books are gone, and I have a big check."

"Do you know who bought the books?" Lovey inquired curiously. "Probably some recluse, like Howard Hughes or someone like that."

"I don't know who he was. I've never seen him before. Some guy named Bill Cantrell. Smart man!"

Jack put his arm around her. "You're a millionaire, Maggie Styles, past owner of Maggie Styles' Antique Barn. You got your insurance dough from the Barn and now this chunk of change. What are you going to do with all that money? Any ideas?"

"Yeah, I think I know," Maggie answered as she looked up into the clear sky.

The next Monday, an article in the Tennesseean newspaper told of how the families of the four missing students in the Abigail Long murder trial had each received anonymous gifts of a million dollars each. The money was gifted from a source only called "The Hope Love Trust."

Jack, Maggie, Lovey, and Wood pulled into the driveway of Wood's house in Florida. Lovey, Wood, and Maggie got out of the car. Jack stayed in.

"You comin' in? You're not leaving are you?" Wood wanted to know.

"No, we gotta go," Jack told Wood.

Maggie hugged them both. "Take care, Dad. I love you; you know that."

"Aw yeah, I figured. Hey, let me know if you decide to start another Antique Barn. I got a garage full of a new start!" Wood offered with a laugh.

Lovey came over to the car window where Jack was sitting and said in her Natalie Schafer voice, "Jack, daaaaahling, I'd just adore it if you came back to see us. It won't be the same without you."

Wood erupted in laughter. "Man, I love it when she does that!"

Jack and Maggie left the driveway and headed down the flat Florida road. Maggie leaned up against Jack. As the sun was setting over the ocean, Jack pulled over to the side of the road to watch it slowly disappear.

"It was a good thing you did for those families, Maggie."

"Yeah, it felt good," she admitted.

"There is one thing we do have to clear up," Jack began cautiously.

Maggie studied him and asked, "What thing?"

"You said you were going to buy a cabin from me if I took you to Florida," Jack reminded her with a smile.

"Oh, I did say that didn't I?" She confessed. "You still in that line of work?"

"Not really. But I'll settle for a steak outside Little Rock. There's a Marriott behind Olin's Steak House I'm rather fond of."

Jack leaned in, kissed Maggie and then the two drove away down the coastal highway.

It's funny how new beginnings nearly always start with a sunset.

ABOUT THE AUTHOR

Wil Hodge was born a "word man." He started out as a teenager writing love notes and poems to his girlfriend. As an adult, this creative passion led him to a guitar named Guilda and a huge body of songwriting work that continues to grow.

Eventually, Wil discovered other musical gifts and created a commercial recording facility in Smyrna, Georgia. For twenty years, he served as a producer and recording engineer for bands, vocalists and other songwriters.

Also a recording artist, his cds, "A Big Gotta Do Done Did, Applewood: Backwoods Lovosine, See What I Hear (With Ryan Almario) and "Place Your Bet," can be purchased on most streaming platforms.

Wil is proud to present his first series of books, "The Dark Ledger" and "The Ghost of Bethel Church." He hopes the intrigue of historical references and paranormal undertones, combined with quirky characters, will draw you into his twisting, turning adventures.

Wil is an avid motorcyclist who lives in Marietta, Georgia with his wife Karla (the girlfriend), and their highly creative daughter Amelia.

He can be contacted at wil@wilhodge.com

www.ingramcontent.com/pod-product-compliance
Lightning Source LLC
Chambersburg PA
CBHW051922110726
47902CB00002B/374